D0550167

'A subversively wicked gift for exploring family tensions' *Independent*

'One of the sharpest and most humorous observers of the human condition writing today for the young' *School Librarian*

'She is translated into 35 languages and has regularly won every major children's literary award in the land ... There are few more influential, or more unfailingly intelligent, authors at work' *Scotsman*

'Anne Fine is brilliant' *Time Out*

Anne Fine has been an acknowledged top author in the children's book world since her first book was published in the mid 1970s, and has now written more than forty books and won many awards for her work, including the Carnegie Medal (twice). Her books can be very funny but there are also often serious underlying themes to be explored with a lack of hypocrisy about the family and honesty about how people can behave.

Children's Laureate from 2001–2003, Anne was honoured both with a Fellowship of the Royal Society of Literature in 2003, and with an OBE. She lives in the north-east of England.

www.rbooks.co.uk

Also by Anne Fine

Published by Corgi Books:

THE BOOK OF THE BANSHEE

THE GRANNY PROJECT

ON THE SUMMERHOUSE STEPS

ROUND BEHIND THE ICE HOUSE

THE ROAD OF BONES

UP ON CLOUD NINE

Published by Corgi Yearling/Doubleday:

BAD DREAMS

CHARM SCHOOL

EATING THINGS ON STICKS

FROZEN BILLY

THE MORE THE MERRIER

For adult readers:

OUR PRECIOUS LULU

ALL BONES AND LIES

FLY IN THE OINTMENT

IN COLD DOMAIN

THE KILLJOY

RAKING THE ASHES

TAKING THE DEVIL'S ADVICE

TELLING LIDDY

For a full list, and for further information about Anne and her writing, see:

www.annefine.co.uk

ANNE FINE

The Stone Menagerie

CORGI BOOKS

THE STONE MENAGERIE
A CORGI BOOK 978 0 552 55994 2

Published in Great Britain by Corgi Books,
an imprint of Random House Children's Books
A Random House Group Company

First published in 1980
Revised edition published by Corgi 2009
1 3 5 7 9 10 8 6 4 2

The Random House Group Limited supports the Forest Stewardship Council
(FSC), the leading international forest certification organization. All our titles
that are printed on Greenpeace-approved FSC-certified paper carry the FSC
logo. Our paper procurement policy can be found at
www.rbooks.co.uk/environment.

Set in12/16pt La Gioconda by
Falcon Oast Graphic Art Ltd.

RANDOM HOUSE CHILDREN'S BOOKS
61–63 Uxbridge Road, London W5 5SA

www.kidsatrandomhouse.co.uk
www.rbooks.co.uk

Addresses for companies within The Random House Group Limited can be
found at: www.randomhouse.co.uk/offices.htm

THE RANDOM HOUSE GROUP Limited Reg. No. 954009

A CIP catalogue record for this book is available from the British Library.

Printed and bound in the UK by CPI Bookmarque, Croydon

For Jake, who loved it first time round

Chapter 1

Ally rocked on his heels at the hospital window, fists clenched at his sides, thinking over the row with his mother. Considering some of the quarrels they'd had, it wasn't so dreadful, but still he was smarting. He thought her unfair and upsetting and rude, with no thought for his feelings.

He'd keep thinking back on it over and over, he knew, feeling rotten and childish and guilty. On bad days he did. She could make him feel awful with just a few tart, scolding words, yet the very same thing on a good day he'd not even notice at all.

He wouldn't go back to his chair so he stood at the window, his nails digging into his palms.

Forcing back all the signs that she'd had him near tears once again, he stared balefully at her reflection, which shone in the glass. He could see she was covering up for him now, glossing over his sullen jerk back from the table that had slopped half the tea from their cups into Aunt Chloe's lap.

'. . . simply one of his moods,' she was whispering to Chloe as she and his father mopped at her wet dress with their napkins and tissues. 'I'm sure he'll be quite all right soon.' But she kept glancing anxiously over her shoulder to check on his scowls in the very same glass pane through which he was glowering at her.

He refused to turn round and come back. But as soon as his first rush of temper was over he managed a peaceable shrugging of shoulders.

She saw it, and said in return to him, via Aunt Chloe: 'It wasn't *entirely* his fault.'

Ally sighed, loosening his fingers and sliding them back in his pockets. There were two steps to feeling all right again after a quarrel, and this was the first. She was no longer angry with him.

It was harder to stop feeling angry with her. In a way she was right when she talked about 'one of his moods'. Though the feelings he had were not new, they now swept over him with a violence he'd not had to cope with before, making him seem the quarrelsome one.

Before, if they started a row, it was always her picking on him. She was always the one who complained, or who walked around nagging, or yelled. Left alone, Ally always felt fine.

In the last few months, Ally had sensed things were changing. And now it was quite often he who spoke sharply, or broke their frayed peace by resisting some plan she had made. He could no longer bear someone else running parts of his life, and although she meant well and she was often right, he just wished she would leave him alone.

Still, on some days, they got along well. But on others he felt she built cages around him, then handed him buns through the bars. She couldn't say one tiny thing on those days without making him feel all churned up, and like running away. He had daydreams of going to sea. He knew he was stuck, what with school and exams and the flute. But he still dreamed of sailing away, out of sight, like Columbus. It always consoled him somehow.

He let it console him right now. He rocked

back and forth on his heels and stared out of the hospital window across the wide lawns, as if they were uncharted seas. A shanty he'd learned on his flute started up in the back of his mind and he whistled it, slightly more cheerfully, under his breath as his eyes roved all over the grounds and his spirits quite steadily lifted.

'See?' He could hear through the shanty his mother's soft whisper. 'He's better now, Chloe. He's whistling. We can relax.'

He focused his eyes back on his mother's reflection. She wasn't relaxing. All tense on the hospital tea-room chair, she leaned across to pat her twin sister's hand, and Ally wondered for the millionth time why they were wasting so much time by coming to see Aunt Chloe. What was the point? She never smiled. She almost never spoke. She wouldn't even try to explain how she'd become so sad and so defeated that she had ended up in this depressing place. She might as well have been a ghost for all the notice she took of what was said around her. She probably wouldn't care if the three of them stopped coming. Why did they bother? It was such a bore.

He sighed again, letting the sea-song fade into

a tuneless mess. He let his eyes blur too. His parents' grey and warped reflections vanished, and in their place the sweep of tangled under-growth beyond the lake took form.

And something else as well.

Pressing his forehead hard against the glass, Ally began to stare. He'd gazed from this window dozens of times, and never seen anyone down there. But he wasn't mistaken. Even from where he was standing, so very far away and so much higher up, he could still see the figure quite clearly.

She was way across on the overgrown side of the lake, among the massive mounds of bramble bushes. Ally couldn't think how she had made her way down there. He had tried often enough, and had to turn back, stung and muddied, with socks full of prickles, and never so much as a dried-up blackberry to show for his pains.

She had done better than him, that was clear. And now she was digging. Straightening in order to ease her back now and again, the small far-off figure was clearing an earth patch where nobody else ever went, and which only the patients this end, in the tea room, could see.

It was not, Ally thought, the most sensible place for a garden. And she'd dressed in the silliest clothes. She was wearing a skirt that was swirling around and which flapped at her ankles and caught in wide folds on her fork, and then needed a tug to be freed. But she was working steadily all the same, getting a good deal done.

It wasn't the fact that she was digging that surprised him. A lot of the patients gardened, after all. And on the other side of Crispin Hospital, behind the sagging tool sheds, were several large, well-tended vegetable plots with everything in rows and, round them, big bright flower beds aplenty.

No. It was the strange out-of-the-way spot she'd chosen that made Ally watch her so closely and wonder if he could get down there, and which of the patients she was.

Just then his mother startled him by saying, 'Go down if you want.'

He focused back on her reflection, wondering how she could possibly have seen what he was looking at. Of course, she hadn't. She just sat there sipping tea and trying to winkle a word or two out of Aunt Chloe. In any case, you'd have to *look,* like sailors look, to see that far away across the grounds.

Obediently, he nodded in the glass, still staring through, absorbed.

Just then the matchstick figure stooped, her skirts awhirl, to pick a stone, or something else he couldn't see, out from between her fork tines. She moved aside to fling it way across the humps of brambles around her and Ally saw, behind the square of ground that she was working on today, a patch she must have planted weeks before.

This time she really took him by surprise. In huge green letters even he could read from way, way up, she'd grown her own name:

Flora

Chapter 2

It must have taken days to clear and plant. Maybe she'd grown it in letters from scratch and then tidied the edges by weeding until it looked perfect. Or maybe she'd started the five plots as sensible squares and then thought of it later and thinned out the plants in that way as a joke.

There it was now, though – a secret green name tucked away in the wilderness over the lake.

Flora.

He said her name over, to test it, still wondering how she got down there. She must have gone often to get so much work done, yet she'd left not the trace of a path. He wanted to find her and look at the name. Was it planted in kingcups or turnips? For though every letter looked different in thickness and height, there was no way to guess what the plants were.

He hoped she was someone he knew, getting better. It could be Miss Fawdry. She wore those long skirts. Or that lady he'd often seen cry in the hall. Growing your name in green plants, Ally thought, was a fine thing to do. A bit weird to do it alone, in what looked like a cleared patch of jungle. But on the right track.

'Oh, do go on down, if you want,' said his mother behind him. She wanted to make him feel bad for not making an effort to talk to Aunt Chloe. But he could pretend that she meant it. He'd done that before when he couldn't stand more of the tea room.

Except he wasn't sure how he would find the patch of ground. And would this Flora mind? Some patients were thin-skinned and wanted to be left alone. He didn't want to spoil things for her. She'd clearly worked so hard on her small patch of earth already, and it must be a very private thing to make her carry all her tools down there. She could scarcely have chosen a more secret place in the whole of the hospital grounds.

As he stood there, deciding, the sun edged in thin silver slices out from behind cloud. Light swept across the lawns down to the lily-choked lake and lit the small green pads to make them shine like bright coins in a bowl. The shimmer hurt his eyes and, wincing, he turned away.

When he looked back, there was somebody standing beside her. It was hard to believe. He had turned his head for only a moment and who-ever it was had appeared out of nowhere, holding a spade.

'You might as well *go*,' Ally's mother persisted, and added sarcastically, 'Perhaps there'll be some-one to *talk* to down there.'

He scowled out of habit and made up his mind.

Sliding a hand out of his pocket, he lifted it, sailor-style, shading his sun-narrowed eyes. He was whistling the shanty again, not so softly this time. He had landmarks to check before he came down from his lookout: a dead elm mast here and a reef of reeds there. It might turn out hard to find poor shipwrecked Flora once he was down on the wide rolling billows of glassy-green lawn, and she was no longer in sight.

Then, sure things were straight in his mind, he was off – out through the swing doors and into the corridor. Nurse Beddowes scolded as he rushed past the drug trolley. 'No running, *please.*' He saluted her white-coated back until she'd gone round the next corner. 'Aye, aye, sir!'

Then past Mr Treadwell, who stared out forlornly from his favourite crow's-nest at the top of the stairs. Past Dr Barney, and down, down, till he was threading his way through knots of uneasy first-time visitors brightly admiring the patients' artwork on the draughty main deck.

A heave at the swing doors beside the front cabin and out, out on the lawns.

He would have to get round by the straggly end of the great oval lake, for the west side would take far too long and they'd mended the holes in the fence. He followed the gravel paths round, then took off down a side slope.

Already his progress was slower. He was deep into undergrowth. The nettles were fierce. Ally pulled his sleeves over his hands to protect them. He hadn't been this way for ages. After a quick glance behind him, he scrambled over the fence beside the fallen hawthorn, then down the slope towards a narrow strip of what looked like cosseted cropped lawn.

It lay quite flat and still. But twice before, he'd landed with quiet friendly splashes up to his knees in this all too innocent-looking mat of green. This time he wasn't fooled. He pulled up short and sat down some way up the bank, staring down at the belt of duckweed, thinking it out again.

Straight ahead, over the fine-spun treacherous green too deep to wade through, was the wilderness. But no way over. Along the bank one way there lay the lake; along the other, the wide curve of swamp he'd skirted often enough before, craving the blackberries on the other side.

Flora had got there, though. And someone else. So, scrambling to his feet, Ally set off along the bank. He fought his way round twice. His third persistent skirting tired him out and, losing his footing on a greasy slope he'd already trampled flat, he slithered down, feet-first. With nothing firm to grab, he arched himself back with a furious yell, fearing he'd slide on down the slope until he stood waist-deep in water with a skirt of duckweed floating round him.

It never happened. Ally looked down to see his shoes slide to a halt on hidden brickwork, his ankles coated with thick, mucky slime.

He'd found the way across the swamp at last.

Chapter 3

It was the broken remains of an old bridge. Poking beneath the duckweed with a stick, Ally worked out that it must have been built as a wide flight of steps to dam the lake through dry months. The water levels must have changed a good deal since, he realized. Then, in the summer, the top few steps would almost certainly have dried out so you could walk across. But in late autumn, the water would have crept up, step by step, until the day it finally flooded over, first in a few narrow trickles, then in one great wide gush.

A moment later, you would never have guessed that there were steps beneath. And now the backwater lay so full and still that there was nothing to give the secret away.

He hardly thought before he started crossing. The stone felt slimy underfoot, with little cracks. He took his time, telling himself that he was in no hurry – Flora would still be there.

But when he made his last, huge, idiot's leap across the final gap – a leap that would have missed the bank entirely and landed him head-long in swamp – it wasn't her but someone else who caught him, and pulled him up to safety on the bank.

Flora herself was sitting further up the bank, in dark green shadow.

'A very nimble crossing,' she said calmly. 'And a good thing that Riley was there.'

Catching his breath, Ally looked up.

She sat cross-legged, her back quite straight, her multi-coloured skirt spread round her like a patchwork rug. Small bits of twig and shreds of leaf were caught in her hair. There was stuff round her eyes, Ally noticed at once, for it made them look huge and much bluer than his, and as round and wide as could be: a kind of black smudging like a freshly-darkened, one-day-old bruise. She was wearing a frayed velvet blouse which had laces and tassels and bows. There were tiny gold bells in her ears.

Ally just stared at her, quite unabashed, in simple and frank adoration. She was lovely, he thought. Like a daydream of his. Eastern-looking, fancy-dressy, Halloweeny. What his father called 'straight off a broomstick' and his mother, with tight lips, 'unkempt'. She was well worth his scratches and stings and his waterlogged shoes.

Riley, he wasn't quite so sure about. For all that he'd been such a help, he looked a little unfriendly. He had stepped away the moment Ally had regained his balance, and now was glowering at the swamp. He was smaller than Flora – not so much taller than Ally himself. He was dressed, unlike Flora, in quite simple clothes, and he looked rather cleaner than she did.

'It may have been a nimble crossing,' Riley said. 'But it was daft. He could have *drowned*.'

'He didn't, though.' Flora had taken off her boots and was rubbing the mud from her toes as she smiled up at Ally. 'He's here now, safe and sound.'

'Yes,' Riley growled. 'He's here now.'

He didn't mean it in the same way Flora did, and Ally suddenly felt shy. Now that they'd met, he didn't think that either of them came from Crispin Hospital – well, not as patients, certainly – but still he felt that he was interfering in some way.

Spoiling their afternoon.

'It's all right. I'll go back now,' he said sadly, gazing into Flora's large and comforting eyes.

'You've only just come,' Flora said.

When Riley frowned at her, she tossed her head back and the tiny golden bells in her ears tinkled away with a summery, gossamer ring that Ally at once found entrancing.

'I came to see *you*,' he confessed, charmed by the tinkling of the bells into a sudden rush of easy explanation. 'I came to see the name you've planted. I wanted to ask what you planted it from.' He swung round to Riley, who'd clearly been scowling while his back was turned and hadn't had time to stop. 'I didn't come down here to bother you. I only came to look at Flora's name.'

'That bothers me,' said Riley.

Still smiling peaceably, Flora bent down and started lacing up her mud-clogged boots.

'Come on, then,' she said gently to them both.

Chapter 4

The name was further back behind the river than he'd thought, but Flora led them quickly through the thickets and clearings, yanking her skirt from brambles and warning Ally of roots lying ready to trip him.

Standing beside it, Ally was disappointed by the name at first. It wasn't as spectacular as he had hoped. Except for the oddly shaped gaps between the patches, it looked like any other vegetable plot. Only the O stood out in any way. But Flora was so proud of it, she won him round again almost at once.

'Well, there it is!' she told him, gazing at it fondly. 'My name. F for fennel, L for lettuce, O for onions, R for rhubarb, A for artichokes.' She made a face. 'There is a bit of cheating in the **F**. There had to be. No one eats that much fennel. I've filled it out with beans around the edges.'

'*French* beans, though,' put in Riley.

'What about Riley's name?' asked Ally, wanting very much to find out just how close they were. It seemed a subtle way to ask.

'She won't do me,' said Riley, answering for her. 'She's thought about it quite a bit, of course, but says the best she can come up with so far isn't worth all the work involved.' He preened himself visibly. 'Riley's a speciality name in places, you see. What did you say I would be, planted, Flora, my bean sprout?'

'**R** for radishes,' Flora began boldly enough. But then her voice turned wistful. '**I** was for Indian corn. I could cope with the **L** for leeks and **E** for endives easily enough. That still left **Y** for yams, though.'

'I wouldn't bother planting that lot, either,' Ally said, and Riley glared at him.

Suddenly hopeful, Flora asked Ally, 'Well, what's *your* name?'

Riley coughed out a sullen, threatening warning which she ignored. The little golden bells tinkled again.

'Alasdair,' Ally told her, very pleased. 'Alasdair Seton.' They stood together thinking for a while, and Ally spoke up first, spurred into added effort by the nice idea of having Flora plant him. '**A** for asparagus, **L** for lentils, **A** for aubergines, **S** for spinach, **D** for Dutch cabbage . . .'

He trailed off just before the end, when he caught Riley's very nasty look.

'Flora's expecting a child quite soon,' Riley remarked with wintry politeness. 'You may perhaps have noticed her unambiguous shape.'

Ally hadn't, but he did at once now it was pointed out. The skirt looked fuller than it need have done; the bodice looser, higher. He stared down at his shoes, his ears bright red. At least he now knew just how close they were, he thought.

Riley mistook his change in expression for bitter disappointment. 'If only you'd been Ed, or even Tom,' he said, thawing. 'But *Alasdair*! I'm afraid not. The strain upon her health!'

'Ally?' suggested Ally.

'No,' Riley told him, adamant. 'Al's our last

offer.' And he strode all the way down to the **A** on the end of Flora's name in a huff.

Flora laid her strong hand on Ally's arm and comforted him by saying, 'Don't you mind Riley. He doesn't mean to be unkind. He isn't cross with you. He's simply worrying that I might make the baby come too soon if I dig **ALASDAIR**. And yet he's longing for the nine months to be over. He's craving to eat charred and blackened flesh.'

'He wants to eat the *baby*?'

Flora broke into smiles which Riley drove away almost at once.

'I could, too, Flora!' he taunted her malevolently over the rhubarb **R**. 'I could eat anything right now. *Anything*. I certainly could eat all the way through my name in one huge juicy feast. Listen to this, Flora. **R** for roast beef, **I** for Irish stew, **L** for leg of lamb, **E** for escalopes—'

'*Stop* it!' cried Flora, turning pale. '*Stop* it!' She let the fork that she'd been leaning on fall over on the **R** and blocked her ears with her fingers. 'Stop it at once, Riley!'

She sounded quite extraordinarily upset, thought Ally, taking the feebleness of Riley's joke into account. He stared at her and wondered for the very first time if she might be a patient after all. Perhaps Riley was visiting. He didn't have the usual look – not really *duty* but not pleasure either – but then again, there might be something not quite right about him too. They had to get to Crispin Hospital from somewhere . . .

'That's Flora for you,' Riley said to Ally, cheered into sudden good spirits by the undoubted success of his spite. He put an arm around her trembling shoulders. 'Denies me every letter of my very own name, except for **Y**, don't you, Flora, my chickpea?' He squeezed her very gently and added, '**Y** for yak steaks,' just to annoy her more.

Chapter 5

Ally jumped to his feet. 'I've got it! Flora, you're a *vegetarian*! And Riley *isn't*. And he can't leave you to go off cooking steaks in case you have the baby while he's gone! I should have guessed. You're just like my Aunt Chloe, up on the hill. She won't eat meat.'

'We don't say that word here,' Riley informed him, taking up his spade. 'We simply don't use the word "meat". For one thing, Flora thinks that it's more accurate – less euphemistic, shall we say – to call it "hunks of charred and blackened flesh", and for another I can't bear to hear the word, I'm longing for some so.'

He poked the handle end of his spade deep in the blackberry bushes behind him. 'I'll catch some of the baby rabbits in here one day soon, Flora, my mushroom,' he threatened her over his shoulder. 'I will. I will. I very nearly got a mole last Tuesday, using a sharpened trowel.'

'Don't you *dare* get life's blood on my fork!' shrieked Flora, incensed. 'I wouldn't be able to dig any more. Don't you dare stain my fork with life's blood!'

Riley emerged from the bushes at once.

'It's a *spade* that I'm trying to clobber them with,' he said, grinning. 'A *spade*.' He turned to Ally, who was staring, open-mouthed. 'I like to call a spade a spade,' he said, and disappeared again between the mounds of brambles.

Flora smiled now, as if she had known he was teasing her right from the start. She turned back to Ally.

'What's your Aunt Chloe's line on eggs?' she asked.

'I'm not quite sure,' said Ally, wondering. 'I've never seen her eat. She always has lunch just before we come, and supper after we've gone. But Nurse Beddowes did once tell my parents that the kitchen staff can't make head nor tail of my Aunt Chloe's vegetarianism. She'll eat the worst cooked cabbage they send up to her, but won't touch nice fresh bean sprouts.'

'I understand that,' Flora said softly. 'Heavens, yes. I understand that.' A pained and tender look shone in her lovely eyes. 'Bean sprouts are such very *tiny* things,' she mused. 'Vulnerable looking. Like small soft newborn babies.' Her eyes filled and she swallowed. 'Tell your Aunt Chloe that she's not alone. I have a hard time eating bean sprouts, too.'

'Listen,' said Riley, backing out hastily from the large bush in which he'd been thrashing around with his spade, apparently still after rabbits. 'Listen, Flora, my courgette, my sweet tender carrot. You must simply stop *thinking* this way. If you take up with Vegetable Rights, we will *starve*!'

'Nonsense,' Flora said briskly. 'There are still pulses and grains, and nuts and dried fruit.'

Riley persisted, in some agitation. A further restriction of diet for him, Ally saw, was a matter of no small importance.

'His Aunt Chloe,' Riley hissed in Flora's ear as softly as he could, but not quite softly enough, 'his Aunt Chloe, Flora, is staying *up on the hill*. Do you know what that means, Flora, my love, my good angel? Do you know what that *means*? It *means . . .*' – and here, presumably out of deference to Ally's family feelings, he softened his hiss, but nowhere near enough. 'It means that his Aunt Chloe is very likely to be curly-whirly-cuckoo, Flora my cocktail onion. *Cuckoo*. That's what it means.'

'Rubbish,' said Flora. 'She's probably simply depressed. She should have more vitamin B.'

'No,' Ally said firmly. 'Riley's quite right. Aunt Chloe's seriously weird, and hasn't eaten bean sprouts for years.'

Riley spoke his thanks civilly on hearing this and nodded gratefully at his supporter. Smiling, he looked a pleasant enough fellow, and Ally had his first glimpse since they met of how the lovely Flora might have brought herself to think of planting Riley's name right beside hers. Let alone other things . . .

Already Flora was interrupting his train of thought about the coming baby. 'I'm sure your Aunt Chloe has her reasons. But you can't call her weird. Some of us *think* about the way we live our lives. To others we're incomprehensible.'

'Dr Barney says certain foods seem to upset

her,' Ally told them. 'Simply to look at them lying on a plate, let alone eat any.'

'Flora's like that with hunks of blackened flesh,' Riley crowed spitefully. 'Do they have any places coming free?'

'What does Aunt Chloe say?' Flora asked frostily.

'She doesn't,' Ally said. 'Aunt Chloe doesn't speak.'

'Doesn't or can't?' asked Riley.

'Doesn't,' said Ally. 'Well, not for *weeks*.'

And all this talk of her reminded him that he should be getting back in time to say goodbye.

Gathering his courage, he asked the two of them, 'Will you be here next Sunday?'

Riley scrunched up his eyebrows into a dark and nasty look, and glared, just as when they first met.

'Yes,' Flora said promptly, her ear-bells tinkling cheerfully. 'Yes.'

'No,' Riley said, just as promptly and a good deal louder. 'No.'

Chapter 6

Ally bent down to hide his flush of shame and pain at Riley's curt reply. He fumbled with his sodden laces, trying not to mind.

It would have been so nice if they'd invited him. He would have thought about it all week long, but not told anyone. It was, he thought, just too much to expect: someone like Flora to talk to, someone to be with. It got very lonely wandering around in the gardens alone until five, or mooching about in the tea room.

Just as he was about to raise his head, ready to say goodbye, Flora put out her hand and laid it on his arm.

'It isn't *you*, Ally,' she told him gently. 'Please don't think that it's *you*.'

Ignoring Riley's warning scowl with yet another toss of her head and tiny golden jangle, she carried on.

'We're not supposed to be down here at all. Although they fenced this end off, worried about the lake, it's all part of the grounds from long ago when Crispin Hospital was still a country house. And so we're trespassing. We're not patients or visitors or staff. We simply *live* here.'

'Change those words round,' Riley suggested bitterly. 'To "We live simply here." *Too* simply, some might think. I do, for one. As for the word "live" . . .' He sighed histrionically. 'You should leave that word out. You can't, in all fairness, really call it a *life*.'

Flora ignored him.

'Riley's not usually horrid,' she went on to assure Ally (who found it hard to credit, but said nothing for her sake). 'His problem is, he can't stop worrying.' She smiled seraphically. 'I can, though. I gave worrying up.'

'What, like meat?' Ally asked, before correcting himself at once. 'Like hunks of charred and blackened flesh?'

'Exactly!' Flora said, clearly delighted with his

progress. 'And after a while, like blackened flesh, you just don't miss it.'

'My mother would,' said Ally. 'She'd fade away. My father sometimes says if she gave up her worrying, she'd be an empty shell.'

'She's like me, then,' said Riley. 'I worry. I would miss it too, just like I still miss meat. And I can't give up two big things at once on a stomach barely lined from time to time with luke-warm greens. So I'll just keep on worrying. If you and Flora don't object.'

Flora smiled fondly at him, offering her muddy hand, which Riley promptly took to gnawing gently rather as if it were some ancient bone.

'What Riley's worried about,' Flora said patiently, 'is *you*, you see. He's worried you could see the name from on the hill. He's worried that you found the way across the swamp. No one else has. It took us weeks, and then we only found it quite by accident when Riley fell in one day.'

'Was pushed,' said Riley.

'Fell in,' insisted Flora.

'Was pushed,' Riley persisted stubbornly.

Flora pretended that she hadn't heard. 'Up until then, and that was May, we were still getting in by climbing over the boundary wall from the main road. But when we found this bridge, we beat a path through from the stone menagerie. It didn't take too long. I think there must have been one anyway, but it had got snarled over.'

Bewildered, Ally looked around. Had she and Riley been down here since May, and several weeks before? It was September now.

'Menagerie,' Flora repeated, misunderstanding Ally's baffled look. 'A sort of little zoo. The seventh earl built it well over a hundred years ago. I think they were a craze.'

'Like conkers,' Riley put in helpfully. 'But a good deal posher.'

'It didn't last for long, though,' Flora said. 'I'm glad it didn't. The earl went broke. Animals cost the earth to feed, so he cut back there. It didn't help him much. Things got so bad he had to sell the house. That's how it came to be a hospital.'

'What happened to the animals?'

'There weren't many left by then. The damp got most of them. And lack of exercise. And unsuitable food. He didn't take a lot of interest in them. Crazes don't last long, do they?'

'No,' Ally said, thinking about the sadly shrivelled conkers his mother ticked him off for leaving in his sock drawer. 'No, I suppose they don't.'

'It's overgrown now,' Flora said. 'But I am happy there – happier than anywhere else I've ever lived.' She waved her hands up to the dappled sunlight. 'And so I want to stay and let my baby grow inside me in all this peace and quiet, away from fussing people and mobile phones and noisy traffic and endless prying questions. I wouldn't want someone to come along and say I have to leave. And that's what Riley thinks will happen if you tell anyone you met us here. That's why he's being horrid. That's what he's worried about.'

'I don't know *why* I worry,' Riley sighed. 'I hate it here. I'd really love to go.'

'He doesn't mean that,' Flora said. 'He trusts me to know what's best for us right now.'

She laid her hand on her belly so Ally knew she meant all three of them.

'So when you've gone, Riley will probably dig up my garden and fling the helpless little onions into the bushes and pull the tangles over once again, so when you say you saw a planted name, nobody will believe you.'

'Oh, no!' cried Ally, horrified. 'Oh, please don't do that, Riley! I'd never *ever* tell.' He willed them to believe him. 'I *know* that I'm the only one who'll notice it. Really I am! Some of the patients do stare out of windows, but they won't *see*. You'd only see if you were *looking*. I've stared out practically every Sunday all through this summer, and only really *looked* today.'

'Carrots!' cried Flora, dismayed. 'The patients should be eating *carrots*. Now please do pass it on.'

'Carrots?' echoed Riley in only half-feigned disbelief. '*Carrots?* Flora's New Blueprint for the Nation's Mental Health! Carrots! I don't believe it!' He reeled back into his bushes. 'Carrots,' he muttered softly. 'Carrots, bunnies.'

'And I won't tell,' said Ally happily, filled with relief. 'I'll never, ever tell.'

'You'd better not,' said Flora. She made a witchy face at him. 'I'll put a curse on you if you do.'

The golden ear-bells pinged, and she and Ally giggled.

'Well, you won't need to,' Ally said.

'I know,' said Flora. 'And so does Riley, really.'

'Oh, yes,' said Riley obediently from inside his bushes. 'Oh, yes. I know now, too.'

'Goodbye,' said Ally, sticking out his hand for her to shake.

She squeezed his palm warmly instead.

'Goodbye,' he said again. 'I'm glad I found you, Flora. And you too, Riley. See you next week.'

He set off whistling down the narrow path that led back to the bridge.

When he looked round, just a few seconds later, to wave at them, they had gone.

Chapter 7

His footsteps echoed down the tea room's pale oak floors. The other visitors raised their eyes to watch him as he passed. Perhaps they guessed he'd be in trouble.

Which would it be? The big freeze? A major guilt trip? Or a serious ticking off? Probably the guilt trip. His mother couldn't get at him for going out. That had been her suggestion, after all, even if she had only said it to try to make him feel rude and unsociable about staying away from the table.

But he'd been gone so long. His father would be restless. He liked to get away well before five. His mother, once the visit to her sister could be ticked off her endless list, would also have begun to fret about the hundred other things she had to do.

And she had reason enough to be annoyed with him. He had been sullen and unhelpful right from the start. He had sat silently, making it clear from the look on his face that he would have much preferred to have stayed home. He had resisted all his mother's efforts to make him talk about his flute lessons – or his new part in the school play. (His best part ever.) He had been careless and clumsy enough to upset the tea in Chloe's lap, then turned his back on them, and disappeared outside.

And yet his mother was always patient enough when it was Chloe. And Chloe didn't try at all. His mother chose the cakes, and poured the tea, and chatted on about the things everyone in the family had done that week. And even though Aunt Chloe hardly lifted her eyes, let alone answered her, his mother was still kind.

Wondering why, Ally dropped in his chair beside his yawning father and stared at his aunt.

She looked so odd, sitting there blinking as usual. The patch of spilled tea on her dress had barely dried. The ruffles round the bottom of her sleeves were now stained brown as well, because she'd kept her hands clasped in her lap. Loose strands of hair slid from beneath the same old hair clip she'd been wearing ever since she came into the hospital. They floated round her haunted face.

'Hello,' he said to her. 'I'm back.'

She didn't even notice. He tried to catch her eye but she was miles away, watching the sunlight flicker through a crumpled cellophane sweet wrapper dropped on the table. Time and again she narrowed her pale blue eyes, then widened them. Over and over.

A nervous mannerism, Dr Barney called it. But for some time now Ally had suspected that Chloe did it quite deliberately, to catch the sparkles of light in just the same way that Ally screwed up his eyes against the street lamps on his paper round on dark wet nights, to make the silver spokes around them dance.

Ally now had a private game for these long dreary visits, of guessing what it was Aunt Chloe was staring at, and what it was about it that caught her interest.

A common thing was sparkles, like the sweet wrapper today. An easy guess, if he were right. Sometimes he thought it was a colour, as on the afternoon Nurse Beddowes switched on the lamp behind Aunt Chloe's chair and made her favourite redcurrant juice turn into blood. Sometimes his aunt's eyes seemed to be drawn by patterns thrown by the tea-time sun through the old window panes into great rippling oblongs on the wall.

Sometimes he couldn't tell.

He always knew she wasn't listening, though. So when his mother also narrowed her eyes – not harmlessly, like her bemused twin sister, but threateningly at him – his whole expression begged for a reprieve. Why did he even have to *try*? Couldn't his parents see that it was *pointless*?

But Mrs Seton was adamant. 'We've *missed* you, Ally. Perhaps you'd like to tell Aunt Chloe just what it was you found so interesting outside to make you stay away so long.'

He couldn't tell them where he'd been. So he said nothing.

His mother pursed her lips. 'I do think

you could make an effort to be more sociable,' she scolded.

He really tried to think of something he could say to his Aunt Chloe. What was his mother trying to nag him into talking about when he stormed off? His part in the school play. He didn't want to tell her about that. She didn't care and wasn't listening.

He'd better think of something else. And fast.

'I've been around the grounds,' he told Aunt Chloe. 'And there's a whole lot more to them than you would think.'

His mother pounced. 'Like what?'

'Just things,' said Ally.

Clearly she was suspicious. 'You were away a very long time.'

Even his bored and sleepy father was looking at him now. Obviously he'd been away so long that they were curious. If he was going to steer them off the topic of where he'd been, he'd have to tell them something else.

Distract them somehow.

He didn't know quite what got into him. But they were happening more and more often now, these strange impetuous moments when out popped something that he hadn't planned.

And it was happening again. Before he could even think for long enough to try to stop himself, he found he'd turned to Chloe, and asked her:

'Want to make a deal?'

Chapter 8

What had he *done*? But there was no going back now. He had better think of something. Fast.

And then it came.

Ally turned to Aunt Chloe. '*Prove* that you missed me,' he challenged, 'and I will cycle over and visit you all by myself next week.'

His mother caught his eye across the table. Her look quite plainly said, 'Watch your step, Ally.'

She thought that he was being insolent. 'Sailing too close to the wind,' as she would call it. But he had started now. And even if he ended up getting a ticking off, he would have shifted his parents safely away from the subject of where he had been.

'The thing is,' Ally leaned across and said to Chloe, 'that Mum believes my sitting in this chair and trying to talk to you might go a little way to cheering you up and making you feel better. And I'm not sure it can. So here's the deal. You show me that you even know that I am here, and I'll come next weekend.'

'Ally!' The look his mother shot him would have frightened stone. And from the way her fingers were scrabbling on her chair arm, he even thought she might be tempted to reach across and slap his face in front of everyone.

But there was no way back now, so he pressed on.

'You see, you never talk. You never even nod or shake your head for an answer. So I'm not sure how you can prove that anything I say even gets through to you.'

His mother half rose in her chair. But mindful of the people sitting round them, James Seton put out a hand to stop her.

Ally pretended that he hadn't noticed. Keeping his tone of voice one of pure innocence, he spread his hands. 'I suppose I could tell you a joke and see if you laugh.'

His father said to him warningly, 'Most of your jokes aren't funny, Alasdair. And take it from me, neither your mother nor I are finding this little scene in the slightest bit amusing.'

'All right,' said Ally. 'I'll be generous and give Aunt Chloe three chances. Three's fair enough. Like Rumpelstiltskin in the fairy tale.' He turned back to his aunt. 'You have to *laugh*, though. So we know you heard.'

He didn't think there'd be a problem. Aunt Chloe wouldn't listen. And even if, by a miracle, she heard the words, she wouldn't get the joke. She was too trapped inside herself to have a laugh. And a good thing, too, because he didn't want to have to spend a few hours with her all by himself next weekend. He would far rather slip away to try to see Flora and Riley. And on the Sunday there was a big rehearsal. He couldn't even think of missing that.

'All right,' he warned her. 'Ready?'

Which were his three worst jokes?

Of course. 'Why do bees hum?' he asked.

'Because they don't know the words,' his father muttered sourly.

'One,' counted Ally.

Apart from blinking at the shiny sweet wrapper, Aunt Chloe hadn't moved.

'What does a giant budgie say?' Ally asked all of them.

Nobody spoke.

'*CHIRRRRRRRRRP!*' bellowed Ally.

The people round them turned to stare and Ally's mother paled.

'Oh, that is *awful!*' Mr Seton groaned.

'Two!' triumphed Ally. He was almost safe.

Aunt Chloe still sat tight.

Ally became expansive. 'This last one's one of my very favourites,' he assured Aunt Chloe. 'I think you'll like it too.'

His mother, irritated by this small, unnecessary cruelty, drew herself up to reach across the table and snatch up the crumpled sweet wrapper that had been lying there all through the visit. Glaring, she crumpled it more tightly in her hand, as if she'd like to do the same to Ally and his so-called sense of humour.

Aunt Chloe flinched. Her face went taut, as if her sister had done something mean, and she looked up. The quick removal of her private treasure brought her attention back, at long last, to her visitors. She realized, looking vaguely round, that Ally had been speaking.

Her eyes met his, briefly and painfully, for the first time that day. He was dismayed. She wasn't going to listen, was she? What if she laughed? That would be his rehearsal up the spout!

'Go *on*, then, Ally,' Nancy Seton said. 'Get on and tell the joke, for heaven's sake. And keep your voice down, please. People are *staring*.'

Inside his head, poor Ally begged his peaky and distracted aunt: please, *please* don't listen. Go back inside yourself. Don't pay a moment of attention to what I'm saying.

'What is the difference,' he asked her coldly, 'between a weasel and a stoat?'

Aunt Chloe drew a little breath and tried to think. He watched her struggling. Her mind slid off, thinking of other things. But Ally's fierce anxious look, which she mistook for hope that she would concentrate, drew her attention back.

She shook her head at last, exhausted.

I'm home and dry, thought Ally. Grinning triumphantly, he gave the answer.

'A weasel's weasely distinguished. A stoat is stoatally different.'

Aunt Chloe did try. He watched her struggling to work out what it was he'd said, and was reminded that, for her as well, these afternoons were just a horrid time to sit and squirm.

Just then, his father got the joke. His sudden shout of laughter filled the room. Everyone round them stared once again as Mr Seton gasped for breath, clutched at his glasses, and roared.

'Weasely distinguished! Stoatally different! Oh, Ally boy, how *could* you?'

He reared back in his chair, howling with glee. His long cramped legs shot out, catching the table leg, and all the teacups, milk jug, spoons and all, fell into Chloe's lap, soaking her for the second time that day.

Her pale blue eyes went wide with shock. Her mouth fell open. Seeing the wreckage in her lap, she gave a nervous giggle.

A funny, torn-off laugh, all on one note.

But still a laugh. It counted.

Poor Ally groaned. He watched as, helpless in her sodden dress, Aunt Chloe was led off.

Just as her sister reached the door, Mrs Seton called out, 'Don't forget next week, Chloe. Ally will see you then,' then turned to smirk at her resentful son. It was, he knew, a punishment for his behaviour. His father, still chortling merrily, passed Ally's mother her coat.

Ally looked up for one more mutinous glare at his annoying aunt to last him through the week. He never managed it. Just as his face was darkening, he saw her stubborn little pause beside the door, the way she slipped out from beneath the nurse's calm, protective arm, and then the tiny, stiff, unpractised wave she made in his direction, singling him out.

Grinning quite broadly at her, Ally waved back.

Chapter 9

The memory of his promise came back to Ally several times during the week. He didn't worry. After all, a weekend was two days, so he could fit in visiting Aunt Chloe *and* the rehearsal. Also, throughout the week he was more busy with the play than he'd expected. All the short practice runs of little scenes they did in breaks and lunchtimes took far, far longer than was planned.

And were more fun. On Friday night, at supper, he told his parents all about the giant fuss during the run-through that day. He leaned across the table, waving his fork excitedly as he described how Susan Lovell, playing the part of Herald, broke in on Pig Mackay's stirring war speech – the very speech that Ally himself had helped Pig write during a dozen lunch breaks.

Sue had one line:

'*Lead, Duke of Clint, thine armies forth!*'

One line. It wasn't much to learn to say correctly. And Pig, as Ally tried to explain, had a slew of lines that everyone looked forward to hearing him declaim, over and over.

'Why? What's so good about them?' Ally's father asked, passing the bread across the table.

Ally's mother frowned. 'Get on and eat your supper, both of you. I don't stand over that hot stove to have you two let all the food go cold talking about nothing.'

Ally shovelled in a forkful of beans and hurried to swallow so he could get on with telling his father about Pig's amazing speech.

'It starts, *"Our enemies' bowels will spill forth from their bellies,"*' he said dramatically over the ketchup bottle.

'Not at the table, please, Ally,' said his mother.

Ally pretended that he hadn't heard.

' *"And stain these daffodils and primroses,*
  Tangling the legs of failing, blood-soaked stallions

some raging army of her own of only one. "Idiot!" she yelled at him. "You big fat fool! You and your stupid raging army have just stamped all over my precious golden locket."'

Ally grinned at his parents. His father's forkful of beans stayed where it was, in mid-air.

'Never!' he said admiringly. 'The things that happen in that school! And who would have thought the girl would be daft enough to wear expensive jewellery under her uniform?'

Ally, quite satisfied with this reaction, turned to his mother. But she had risen to her feet the moment he stopped speaking and now her back was turned. She had begun to clatter plates into a pile by the sink.

'You won't forget about your arrangement with Aunty Chloe at the weekend, will you?'

Ally's face fell. She hadn't even listened. She'd just been waiting for him to finish so she could clear the table. She hadn't heard a word. Really, she might as well be his Aunt Chloe for all the notice that she ever took of what he said.

Or was it something else? Could there be any-thing about the plan to visit Chloe that was niggling her? She'd not come out and say it

57

straight. That wasn't her way. But still he felt like a skater on creaking ice that any moment now might crack into a treacherous jigsaw of jagged swaying pieces he might be lucky enough to tip-toe over, reaching the bank in safety.

Or else slip down between, into the chilling water, to drown.

Chapter 10

Next morning, the minute Ally had finished his share of the cleaning, he slid out of the back door. Dragging his bike from the shed, he turned it upside down and sat beside it with a heap of tools. So long as he kept spinning the rear wheel so that the faint tinny ticking floated in through the window, his mother would assume that he was busy and wouldn't look around for one more little Saturday morning job for him to do.

And it was soothing, sitting there. He liked the steady whirring of the wheel. He liked to watch its inner circle blur to a silvery fog, then sharpen back to spokes again each time the spin slowed.

He needed time to think.

He knew as clearly as if his mother had announced it through a megaphone that some great quarrel was about to break. The storm clouds had been gathering all week, and when he woke that morning he'd found himself, like a small cautious animal, sniffing the wind.

Even though it was Saturday, he'd thought it wiser not to laze about in bed too long. Even before she'd called him for the second time, he'd stepped into the kitchen and said as brightly as he could:

'Good morning, Mum.'

At first, she didn't respond. Her back was turned as she was standing at the sink, rinsing a plate and cup. When, finally, her rather distant greeting came, it was as if she had been wondering whether to kick off with whatever it was that was annoying her, or wait a little longer.

He'd gobbled his cereal much faster than was pleasant, to try to get safely outside. It was, he thought, like sitting at a picnic watching skies darken. And it would come as some sort of relief when the first heavy drops splashed down at last, forcing the run for shelter.

There was no getting out of it now, whatever it

was. Ally knew that from long experience. This ticking off was certainly going to happen.

But for the life of him he couldn't think what he might have said or done to put her in this strangely dangerous mood. He'd scoured his memory and there was nothing. Could it be what he was *about* to do that was annoying her? She didn't *talk* as if that was the case. At least a dozen times she must have said, 'How nice to think your dad and I can do something different this weekend, and still be sure that Chloe will have a visitor,' and, 'You won't forget your promise, will you?' But now he thought about it, every time it had been said in that vague, automatic, slightly nagging way she usually said, 'You won't forget to do your homework, will you?' or, 'Did you remember to bring home your football shirt?' – as if her only real intention was to bring him back from whatever flight of fancy he was floating on, down to the real world.

He couldn't back out now. If he did that, he'd never hear the last of it. His mother would bring it up for months as an example of how his promises couldn't be trusted.

'I'll do my jobs tomorrow, honestly I will,' he'd

plead as some match all his mates would certainly be watching kicked off on television.

'Oh, yes? I've heard that one before,' she'd say, prising the television plug out of its socket and plugging in the vacuum. 'And what about that time you promised faithfully you'd visit Aunty Chloe, and didn't go?'

No doubt she thought that he'd prefer his weekend to himself. But she'd be wrong. If there was even the chance of seeing Flora, then Ally was quite happy to cycle all the way to Crispin Hospital. Riley too, really. And he did not mind spending time with Aunty Chloe, either, if he was honest. Once or twice in the week a picture had come back to him of how she'd stood by the door in her wet dress and sent him that last little wave.

No. He was keen enough to go. But not to-morrow, missing the big rehearsal. Nor did he want to put it off a week. Really, he should have said something to his mother a whole lot sooner.

Last chance if he was going to go today.

Slamming the tyre to a halt, he went back in the kitchen. 'About this trip to Crispin Hospital . . .'

His mother turned. 'Yes, Ally? What about it?'

'Tomorrow's not a good day. You see, we have one of the big rehearsals for the play and—'

'Oh, I see!' It was as if she couldn't even be bothered to listen long enough to hear him out. 'Trying to wriggle out of it!'

He was quite sure that was a smirk across her face. Her voice was scornful. Even her eyes were gleaming in a sort of triumph, as if to say, 'I know you better than you know yourself, and I *knew* that you wouldn't go.'

He found it maddening. It made it easier to sound more firm. 'And so I'm going to visit her today instead.'

His mother stared. 'What, *now*?'

'Yes.'

'On your bike? I thought from the way that you were clanking around outside that there was something wrong with it.'

'No,' Ally said. 'The bike is fine.'

Why was she looking so put out? 'It's a long way.'

'It's not too far. And most of it is cycle paths.'

'You'll have to get off for the dangerous roundabouts.'

What was the *problem* with her? It was as if

she really didn't want him to keep his promise.

'I promise. And I'll use the overpass across the dual carriageway.'

His mother's lips were tight as purse strings. Giving a scornful laugh, she turned back to the cupboard shelves.

'I shouldn't bother, Ally. I bet Aunt Chloe doesn't even remember you said you'd come. And if she does, I shouldn't for a moment think that she'll be bothered if you don't show up.'

He forced himself to keep his voice steady. Why did she *say* these things? Was it deliberately to make him feel as if he didn't matter? Of course it might be true. Yet when Aunt Chloe waved, he'd had this strange sense of companionship, as if she was doing it, not out of left-over, half-remembered good manners, but out of fellow feeling – as though the two of them had some-thing in common. And though the nursing staff were always kind, they did tend to treat Aunt Chloe rather as if she were a child even younger than Ally. ('Come on now, dear. Shall we go back upstairs?') Even through all that blinking, Aunt Chloe could scarcely have failed to realize that Ally found the visits as grim as she did. No doubt his mother was right and things did tend to float out of her sister's mind. And yet it was just possible that she'd been clinging to his reckless promise all through the week.

She might be waiting for him and be disappointed if he backed out – just didn't come.

He stuck his tongue out at his mother's back to give himself the courage to insist. 'Well, I'm still going.'

He saw the muscles tense along her neck.

'Suit yourself, Ally. So long as you're careful on the bike, I don't care either way.'

She wasn't pleased, though. That was obvious. And this was how he and his mother rubbed along all the time now. She'd say one thing, but he could sense that something else was simmering underneath. It was like being small again, hearing himself told yes, yet feeling told no. He could remember padding up to her, always so busy round the kitchen, carrying his paint box. 'Can I do pictures now?'

'Oh, I suppose so,' she would say. But she'd be frowning. Then there would be a host of irritable orders. 'First, get an apron, Ally. No, not that one. That one's too good for paints. And you'll need newspapers. No, more than that. And use a *plastic* beaker for the water. That glass might break. No, not at *that* end of the table, Ally. I'll be rolling pastry there soon.'

It just went on and on. And usually in the end he'd given up and gone to do jigsaws quietly, out of the way.

Now he was older he could understand why she'd been in two minds about the spills and messes that she'd seen coming when she had so many things to get done. But this was different. It was as if she didn't know her own mind. He had the feeling she'd be almost pleased if he cried off – even though that would show that he was still so young and irresponsible that his announcements and his promises could not be trusted.

Perhaps that was it! She'd been a mother for so long, perhaps it unnerved her to think he might now be grown up enough to spend an afternoon alone with her strange sister. That he was getting bigger, taller, stronger and more sensible. Not quite as shy as he had always been before.

That one day, even, he'd be up and gone, to live his own life – no longer on a string.

What better time to start? Strangely elated, he

slid his fingers in his pocket and round his phone. Turning his back, he laid it quietly on top of the bits and pieces in the little cluttered pot on the dresser. She'd see it later when she went for her car keys – or, if she tried to keep tabs on him, when it rang.

'Well, then,' he told her firmly. 'I'm off now.'

'I want you back by six.'

'I won't be late, I promise.'

His mother made a little face as if to say, 'I'll believe that when I see it.'

And Ally made a private vow, to spite her. He would *not* be late.

Chapter 11

Nurse Beddowes didn't seem at all surprised that Ally had come on his own. 'Off to the tea room?' she asked. 'Or will I tell anyone who asks that you two are in the garden?'

Ally gave Chloe a look, but she was clearly paying more attention to the buttons on her cardigan than to the question.

Ally decided. 'I think we'll be in the garden.'

'Righty-ho.'

Nurse Beddowes pressed the button for the lift, but Chloe was already making for the stairs. Ally took after her. She didn't speak to him the whole way down – but then again, she didn't seem to be 'not speaking' either. They just went down companionably – like an old married couple, Ally thought, who didn't feel the need to think of things to say to one another.

Out in the grounds, it was another matter. With all that space around the two of them, he felt obliged to talk. He didn't know much about flowers or plants, so in the end, just as his mother had suggested the week before, he told her all about the play. It wasn't hard. She asked no questions and she didn't smile, but seemed content just to keep wandering in and out between the flower beds and on around the building to the back.

There, creeping between the patients' vegetable plots, apparently stealing spinach, they came across a crouching figure Ally recognized at once.

'Riley!'

Riley drew himself up, flushed with embarrassment, and hurried over. 'I don't feel guilty,' he assured them, riddled with guilt. 'Most of it goes to seed. Also, I'm very careful to take the same amount from everyone, even though Flora says the spinach from the plot on the end is unquestionably the best.'

'Taking a leaf out of Goldilocks' book,' said Ally happily. 'A spinach leaf!'

Riley's lip curled in feigned contempt at Ally's witticism. He turned his back on him. 'Is this your Aunty Chloe?'

He took her soft limp hand and kissed it extravagantly. Aunt Chloe looked up, startled.

'I'm pleased to meet you, madam,' Riley said. 'Flora's been talking about you all week. And vitamins. And carrots. She wants to have a heart-to-heart. Lend you some pamphlets. Why don't you come for lunch?'

Aunt Chloe's face stayed blank. Thinking of Flora's pretend curse, Ally said softly, 'I thought you didn't want people to *know*...'

'No more I do,' said Riley hastily. 'Certainly not. Especially with stolen goods lying around in salads.' He waved the bunch of spinach airily. A small black insect fell from its depths onto his hair, and started crawling laboriously towards his ear. 'But you told us Aunt Chloe never spoke.'

'You can't depend on it,' said Ally darkly, remembering the laugh and little wave.

Riley did not seem worried. Already he was sliding his arm round Chloe's waist.

'You'll take to Flora's cooking, probably,' he coaxed her shamelessly. 'Being more interested in what it's made of than how it ends up tasting. And maybe later you and I can make a deal. I'll creep up here to the hospital after dark with beetroot quiche, and spinach stew, and thin stalk soup, and all the other things she's starving me to death on. And you, in return, can pass me lumps of wholesome, nourishing Spam out through the window.'

'Aunt Chloe's on the top floor,' Ally said.

Riley looked most concerned.

'You're not,' he said. 'Are you?' He shook his head. 'One wonders how they suppose people can ever come back down to earth, stuck that high up.'

Aunt Chloe hadn't heard. A rustle and a wing-flutter deep in a nearby bush had caught her attention. Before Riley finished speaking, she was already wandering off. But Riley caught her hand and pulled her gently back on the gravel path.

'Mustn't be late,' he scolded her. 'You know as well as I do, braised Brussels sprouts just can't *wait.*'

Chapter 12

Down at the swamp, Riley knelt to unlace Aunt Chloe's worn grey sneakers and, knotting them together, slung them round his neck along with his own shoes.

'If you don't concentrate,' he told Aunt Chloe sternly, 'you'll probably fall in.'

'And *drown*,' said Ally, hoping to stress the point. He felt responsible, and dreaded something awful happening. 'The pills they give her make her dizzy sometimes,' he said to Riley.

'She'd better hold our hands then,' Riley said.

He led her carefully onto the hidden bridge. She looked down once in great astonishment, just as her feet got wet, as if, although she'd seen the water lying there and known that water was wet, it still came as a shock.

Ally, behind her, thought a little nervously that he was always getting bits of his Aunt Chloe wet in one way or another. She'd probably contract pneumonia after this week, and die because of him.

The water felt chilly and, in bare feet, much slimier than before. Strange and disturbing swampy smells kept wafting up. He had a sudden notion of how peculiar the three of them must look – a line of sideways water-walkers, ankle-deep, all holding hands, the bridge invisible.

Halfway across, without a warning, Chloe drew up short, pitching her helpers into surprised imbalance. She snatched her hands away from both of theirs and stood, quite unconcerned, as Riley's flailing arms rocketed both pairs of shoes around his neck into the murky water.

'Hey!' Riley said. 'Watch out!'

But he was talking to himself. Ignoring both of them entirely, Aunt Chloe had risen like a dancer on her toes and swivelled round to face the coming bank.

'Chloe—'

But she had stretched her arms out gracefully. The ruffled sleeves fell back, revealing thin white scars down both her wrists. Her hair caught in the breeze. Ignoring their waving hands, Aunt Chloe stepped on with the utmost confidence, pointing her toes to search out the brickwork underneath, and moving so steadily that Riley, who was still in front, had to move fast to stay ahead of her, and ended up windmilling his arms as he leaped off the last of the uneven brickwork onto the bank.

By the time he'd regained his balance, Aunt Chloe had stepped safely and elegantly off the bridge.

Riley reached out to pull Ally up to join them.

'Is everyone in your family given to sudden suicidal turns whilst crossing water?' he asked sarcastically.

Ally saw no reason not to defend himself and his relations. 'She was managing a whole lot better than you were.'

Riley fished round in pond weed for the sinking shoes. Once they were safely landed he turned to look at Chloe. But after her short display of physical confidence, she'd shrunk away again inside herself, and now stood feebly blinking at sunlight dapples on the leaves.

Riley pulled on his shoes and Ally watched as he made huge and clumsy bows with sodden laces. Calmer now, Riley rose and handed Chloe's dripping sneakers back to her. She looked at them as if they were not hers and laid them tidily on the ground, as if she was about to walk away from them.

Then, deftly bending like an acrobat, she put them on.

'She must take classes,' Riley dropped behind to whisper to Ally. 'No one's that bendy naturally.'

'She's younger than you think,' admitted Ally. 'She's only looked this old since she's been in here. I think that it's because she won't wear anything except grey clothes and keeps that granny-style grip stuck in her hair. When she's all right, she looks quite different. She's a real surprise.'

Riley said ruefully, 'I wouldn't doubt it, Ally. Already she's surprised me quite a bit.'

He led his lunch guests on, between the tangles under the ancient trees, while Ally dutifully brought up the rear to make sure they didn't accidentally lose Aunt Chloe on the way. Ally had never been in such dense woods before. Even the brambles interwove above their heads and sometimes underfoot. The pond-green tunnels of beaten path sucked them in and along, past the turn-off to Flora's name, and round strange twirling bends, over soft, rotting planks that lay across thin streams, and on and on, until the wild and briar-choked old spinney became, in front of them, as dark and impenetrable as a real wall.

Daydreaming fairy tales, Ally heard himself muttering, 'I could *hack* my way through to rescue Flora.'

Too loud. Ahead of him, Riley had come to a halt. '*What* did you say?' he turned to ask dangerously. '*What* did I hear you say?'

'Nothing,' said Ally.

'Listen,' hissed Riley. 'Listen here, Little Prince Alasdair.' He pulled him nearer over the mossy roots and crumbling bark and pressed his face close. 'You have less cause to think yourself the Sleeping Beauty's handsome rescuer than your Aunt Chloe has to take upon herself the role of Principal Acrobat.'

'Sorry,' said Ally.

Riley's scowl deepened. 'And don't forget, if

anyone needs rescuing from this forsaken thicket, it's *me*, not Flora.'

'Quite right,' Ally soothed.

'Not to *mention* the fact that if you and I just happened to be in the very same jumble sale, Flora would definitely buy me first.'

'I'm sure she would,' said Ally.

He scuffled out of Riley's grip and stared, embarrassed, straight ahead of him. And so he came to see the gates at last, realizing only then that they had, indeed, come up against a wall.

In places it could not be seen at all, so heavily shrouded was its crumbling stonework by sprawling, riotous creepers. If it weren't for the gates, which stood ajar, the wall itself might have remained unnoticed, hidden as well as it was within its own dark green protective girdle.

The gates were slim and high, and made of iron wrought into intricate swirling patterns like writhing coal-black serpents. Someone had pulled the creepers from them recently. Only a few slim energetic tendrils, pale green with whitened tips, looped up the lowest coils.

Aunt Chloe shrank back. Ally took her hand. He thought about the way the gargoyles on the

church had frightened him when he was young –
still did on dark wet nights. Squeezing her fingers,
he pulled his aunt through behind him and, once
inside, looked around in wonder.

'Is this it, Riley? Is this where the animals
were kept?'

Riley beamed proudly, spread his arms out
wide and said in a proprietorial manner:

'Yes. This is it. We think of it as Vegetable Hall.
The Stone Menagerie.'

Chapter 13

The silent empty cages lay in a ring around him in strange green underwater light trapped by immense tall trees. Huge frondy arches interlaced overhead, as if to turn the clearing into a pale and shadowy goldfish bowl.

Ally let go of Chloe's fingers, and stepped out onto the lush grass.

Each cage was built of thick grey stone, its facing side striped with great rusting bars. Square cages alternated round the ring with oblongs. Breaking the circle twice were two deep pits. 'For bears, almost certainly,' said Riley, pointing down. And everything was cloaked in deep, disguising green: mosses and ferns and grasses, creepers and briars.

I might have walked right through, thought Ally, and not noticed it.

The circle had a mournful, half-deserted feel, as if the animals who lived and died there had not wholly gone. 'The lions must have hated it!' cried Ally suddenly, seeing them there behind the bars, their great black noses heavy on their paws – that doped, half-living look. 'All cramped up! No real sun!'

'It wasn't quite so bad then,' Riley comforted, tilting his head to gaze up. 'The trees hadn't spread so far. But, yes, they must have hated it. All of them, not just the lions. I've thought about them such a lot since we moved in.'

He strode around the circle, pointing in every cage. 'The lions. Tiger. Elephant – if they could keep one long in that dank hole. Here in this pit, the bears. Turtles. A camel, perhaps. A zebra. Some maddened, pacing leopard. And here, saddest of all, the staring, hopeless monkeys.'

'Please stop,' cried Ally, terribly upset. He felt his legs were buckling under him, and sat down on the grass. The tears rolled down his cheeks, his shoulders shook. He cried and cried. 'Riley,' he sobbed. 'We went to a little zoo as small and cramped as this last year on holiday.'

'Well, you'll know better next time, won't you,' Riley said. 'You mustn't fret about the ones you've seen so far. Pennies take time to drop.'

'Not this one,' Ally told him ruefully.

'Come on,' said Riley, pulling him to his feet. 'Come and see Flora. Flora will cheer you up. She'll tell you just how many little pink piglets' lives you'll save each year if you become a vegetarian, and how to boycott bullfights and zoos and circuses.'

'Circuses?'

'Some of them,' Riley said. 'The foreign ones that still use animals. Just think about it.'

'My parents say that they enjoy doing their tricks,' Ally suggested weakly. He looked up, full of hope.

'Come off it, Ally,' Riley told him coldly. 'Some of the dogs, perhaps. Maybe the ponies. But tigers? *Tigers?* Haven't you ever *looked* at a tiger, Ally?' He saw the downcast face and put his arm round Ally's shoulders. 'It's time to think about these things yourself, you know. You can't be comforted all through your life with lies your family told to cheer you up when you were small and saw things all too clearly.'

'I suppose so,' said Ally.

He wiped the tearstains from his cheeks and turned to check on Chloe. She was still staring around, appalled, at the stone cages. As Riley wandered off in search of Flora, Ally looked at his aunt with growing interest and an inkling of respect he'd never felt before. She was like Flora, never eating meat. He wondered when she had decided that. She hadn't picked it up from family, that was for sure.

He wondered if she'd gone off circuses the way she shrank from meat. She and her sister, had they once sat together on a wooden bench under the vaulted canvas walls of one of those old-fashioned circus tents? Had they laughed at the clowns, delighted in the glitter and spangles, gasped in sheer wonder at the glistening aerial bodies, admired the golden balls that spun from hand to hand in swooping patterns, half hoping one might even drop to prove the magic real? Had she and his mother nudged one another in delight as they nibbled candy floss, and giggled when the tiny tasselled pony scooted beneath the great carthorse's belly and popped out, hooves a-flying, the other side? Nancy and Chloe Seton, quite alike in thinking everything that night was wonderful.

But then, had Chloe watched alone throughout the interval while men with silver braiding on their sleeves hoisted the cast-iron caging out of the shadows and hooked it in a circle, spreading the vast grey cone of heavy netting over the top? Perhaps she had already fallen silent by the time Nancy hurried up the steps between the buzzing, jam-packed families, holding the ice creams high above her head.

And when the first great lion padded out from the cage tunnel into the floodlit ring, and blinked, and shook his heavy powerful head and stared at her with hollow amber eyes, did she look down and press her fingers hard into her ears and eyes until they bruised, trying so hard never to hear the vicious gunfire whip-crack, or see the splendid animal flinch and jump, and do the stupid things they'd forced him into doing?

That's when it started, perhaps. She had preferred to slide away inside herself, and see the lion pounding over a sun-drenched plain, uncaged, alone.

When she looked up, a short while later, hearing the clang of heavy bars being removed at last, was her face pale and drawn as it was now; the ruffles round her wrists stained from the dripping ice cream, her socks in folds round her thin ankles, loose strands of mousy hair floating around her peaky, haunted face?

'You didn't ever go again, did you?' he said. 'First circuses, even before that kind of thing was banned. Then zoos, however good and kind they claimed to be. And, not long after, you gave up eating meat as well. I bet you found it hard to tell them why. They're not an easy lot to hold your own against, if all the rows I have with Mum are anything to go by. I bet you soon gave up and just kept quiet.'

He shuffled his feet in leaf-mould, thinking of things to come.

'I think I'm more robust than you are, really,' he told her after a while. 'I've had a lot more practice being difficult. I'm going to dig my heels in when things like this come up for me. Refuse to budge, like you. But tell them why. I think it might be better in the long run.'

She hadn't heard him. Even when he went over

to take her hand, it wasn't Chloe he was comforting. It was himself.

'Come and see Flora,' he murmured softly. 'Yes. Come and see Flora. Flora will cheer you up.'

Chapter 14

Since none of the cages was sunny enough to sit in, they ate outside. 'Cages are fine for suppers,' Riley remarked. 'Cosy by candlelight. They're not too bad for breakfast, either. But lunch and afternoon tea . . .' He eyed the iron bars. 'It sort of *grates*,' he said, grinning apologetically.

'Doesn't *mesh* with the mood,' chimed in Ally.

Flora was kind enough to laugh at his joke too, he noticed. The golden bells in her ears tinkled away and Aunt Chloe giggled.

She can't have got the puns, though, Ally thought. She'd have to be paying a whole lot more attention than she usually does to what is said. It must be something else inside herself. Nevertheless, he thought he'd watch his aunt more closely after this – this and the wave. You never knew. Perhaps that brilliant balanced walk across the bridge showed she was cheering up.

'Soup?' Flora distracted him, passing a cracked grey bowl of steaming greenish-browny liquid, with wilting flecks of something a slightly paler green floating around on top.

'That's parsley,' Riley said, pointing. 'I stole that too, to eke the soup round four. Give it some *body*.'

Ally poked tentatively with his spoon. Strange black things just like mouse-droppings swirled to the surface.

Ally's face fell.

'Soup, Riley,' Flora said. Firmly she kicked out of his reach the pile of juicy grass stalks he'd just laboriously collected. 'I *wish* you wouldn't spoil your appetite just before every meal.'

Riley reached forward to lift the tin bowl Flora had put down for him, then yelped in pain and sat there miserably sucking his scalded fingers.

'It's far too hot to touch right now,' Flora informed him just a moment too late, ladling soup into Aunt Chloe's bowl.

Relief transparent on his face, Riley pulled

down his sleeves to protect his hands as he slid the bowl behind him, out of the way. Ally could see the grass blades shrivelling as the soup slopped over.

'Of course,' added Flora – a little tartly, Ally thought, unless you bore in mind that eating as a topic had been the source of endless wrangling between these two, 'of course, if you just leave it sitting there too long as usual, it will get too cold.'

'That's life for you.' Riley sighed heavily. He lay back on the grass and stared at the leafy canopy above. The sunlight, spitting through the tiny holes, flecked him all over. 'There in a nutshell you have Life, Aunt Chloe.'

It suddenly occurred to Ally that while Riley stolidly ignored the soup that Flora had been slaving on all morning, and chatted away vaguely, now was his first big chance to worm his own way into the lovely Flora's confidence and affections.

She sat, serene as ever, on the grass, her hair and face, like Riley's outstretched body, speckled with dancing lights. She'd done her crinkly leaf-strewn hair in childlike plaits today, and sat chewing the ends, watching the three of them as they sat eyeing, quite suspiciously, the contents of their bowls.

She might, he thought, be waiting. Waiting for compliments on her nice soup.

A steady supping, Ally thought. Appreciative murmurs as he spooned. A polite but quite unhesitating request for more, should there be any going. And later, after the pudding (if there was one), a calm, sincerely stated resolution to turn vegetarian.

That should do the trick.

He'd give the right impression: imply that with himself there'd be no feeble-minded hankering after charred flesh, no weak relapses into roasted mole, like the ones Riley suffered.

Look at him, Ally thought contemptuously. Lying stretched out, leaving the soup Flora had given him to cool from hot to tepid while he chewed desperately on her bare toes instead.

Ally watched Riley's warped carnivorous gestures with icy disapproval. *He* wouldn't act like that when he was 'in' with Flora. He'd ask to see her pamphlets. All of them. He'd take them home with him at night and read them all, after he'd done his homework. Return them to her one by one. Discuss the points with her. She'd soon see he was more her type than rabbit-hunting Riley. It wouldn't take too long.

And then, in a few months, when he was older . . .

His scheme hatched out, he stirred his soup to whirlpools, blowing energetically. The more heated his hopes, the more that Ally prayed his bowl of soup would cool before Riley's. It smelled a little strange, and vague and indistinct reminders of the swamp came wafting through his mind. But Ally was determined that it would taste delicious.

Lifting the spoon, he took his first enthusiastic mouthful of Flora's soup.

Chapter 15

He found it hard to swallow. Even though manners dictate quite unequivocally that there was no alternative – he could not simply spit it out again onto the grass – he found it hard to swallow. And as he struggled, cheeks and eyes bulging, he looked at Riley with a new respect. An awe-struck admiration.

This man had stayed with Flora for several months. It must be almost nine, at least, thought Ally, as his eyes strayed to Flora's swollen belly. Riley had stayed alive for several months on Flora's food, with only the odd hard-won hedge-hog and bartered hunk of institution Spam to keep him going.

Ally could recognize true merit when he saw it.

He sat, a little gravely, on the grass, paying his silent inward tribute to Riley's strength of purpose, his mouth still filled with slimy, sickening soup, his throat rebelling fiercely against the longed-for swallow, the one hope of release.

He ceded Flora up, once and for all. He would compete no longer, he decided. Flora was Riley's. Riley could eat her food. Riley had *earned* her.

He burned with admiration for the man and his restraint and courage. He'd swallow for *his* sake.

'*Glurrrp.*'

He made the noise as quietly as he could. Release was earned. The soup slid down. It tasted even worse than he had feared, and Ally's initiation into a blind, wild, hero-worship of Riley took place right there and then.

Tilting his bowl as unobtrusively as possible, he watched the sour green mess dribble its way, painfully slowly, into the grass. Dust unto dust, thought Ally. Ashes to ashes. He'd seen more appetizing liquids drip from his father's lawn-mower and stain the garage floor.

'Would you like more?' asked Flora

comfortably, noticing his bowl was empty. 'I did make seconds all round.'

'No thanks,' said Ally, ashen-faced, as calmly as he could. 'First rate, but no.'

'Go on,' Flora persisted. 'There's plenty left.'

She tipped the pan to show him. He felt a powerful spasm writhe in his shrinking stomach.

'No, Flora. No. No more, thanks,' Ally said.

'Don't press him, Flora, my cucumber slice,' Riley now interrupted, his face quite bland, his eyes all innocence. 'He looks as pale as a maggot. He did mention on the way down here that he was feeling queasy. He didn't really want to stay for lunch. He said he wasn't hungry.'

'Yes, really, Flora,' Ally pitched in gratefully. 'I'd just as soon throw up as eat.'

'Can I have all his seconds, then?' Riley asked, swelling with sheer bravado. 'I *love* this soup.'

Ally's wide eyes glistened with wonder. This man was noble, dazzling, awe-inspiring. A god among men! He felt for him a fervent gratitude – taking his seconds! Willingly! Unasked! – a deep, deep obligation.

He watched, shyly and reverently, as Flora

tipped the pan and filled Riley's bowl up to the brim with Ally's share of soup.

There wasn't much that anyone could do to repay Riley properly for such self-sacrifice and thoughtful generosity.

An idea came at last.

'Look, Flora! Look!' he cried. 'Up in that tree behind you! A magpie, Flora!'

Flora turned to look. Aunt Chloe's spoon hand froze, and she too turned her face upwards. But Ally had no time to be surprised that Chloe paid attention to what he said. *Quick*, his pale anguished look implored his hero. *Quick*, Riley. Tip it out *now*, there on the grass behind you, while she's not *looking*.

But Riley sat quite still, tranquilly smiling, cradling his bowl and affecting not to understand the point of Ally's frantic gestures. And when Flora turned back, a little frown of disappointment on her face because the magpie must have flown without her seeing it, he cheered her up at once, dispensing with the bent old spoon to raise the bowl to his lips and drink the lot without a pause, making happy and appreciative noises.

He held the bowl out, empty but for some pale

green smears around the edge, for all of them all to see.

'I really *love* this soup,' he quite outrageously bragged again to Ally, not unaware that he had won his way through to some subtle kind of triumph concerning Flora. 'That parsley adds the little *je ne sais quoi* it needed. Don't let me take it all, though. No again, Ally? How about Aunty Chloe?'

'More?' Flora offered her, scraping around inside the pan with her huge wooden ladle. 'Would you like more?'

'Yes, please,' said Chloe, holding out her bowl. 'Yes, please, Flora.'

Ally gazed at his aunt in some mystification. Not only was it still quite startling to hear her voice, but this was, he realized, the third thing in a row that she'd heard somebody say first time, with no real prompting. And as for her response, she'd sounded little short of eager.

He watched Aunt Chloe, baffled and appalled, as she spooned briskly from her bowl, finishing the last of the soup. She downed the foul, disgusting stuff with relish, even the small black things that lurked in its depths.

Not only that, he thought, doubly astonished now he came to think of it, she hasn't done her funny blinking act once since we came down here. Not once.

Chapter 16

All afternoon, Ally wandered around the stone menagerie, admiring almost equally Flora's inventiveness and Riley's fortitude.

Inside the tiger's cage, Flora had built a wooden platform that could be raised against the wall in daytime and let down at night to keep their sleeping bodies off the chilled stone floor.

'That's clever,' Ally said. He lay on the bedroll Flora had thrown down to show him how the whole arrangement worked and felt his bones grind against wooden slats. 'It's also *hard*.'

The lion's cage particularly impressed him. Flora had chosen to use this as a kitchen because it had protection from the wind. She'd built a most ingenious set of small brick ovens round an open fire. Across the top, bars from the turtles' subterranean entrance made an unsteady grill on which pans wobbled. The feeding trough from yet another cage stood close at hand, filled with dank water to douse the fire in case of accidents.

Boxes in one dry corner held their meagre stores.

'What have you got in there, then?' Ally asked.

'Brown flour,' said Riley gloomily. 'Wheatgerm and brewer's yeast. Crunchy granola. Eight types of bran. Pamphlets. You know the kind of thing...' He looked down at his feet. 'And, of course, trespassers.'

Ally looked down as well. A steady trail of large, well-nourished ants led from the outside of the cage across the floor into the boxes; and Ally saw across the worn slabs of stone the glistening dried silver tracks of long-gone slugs.

'Flora discourages slugs, don't you, my chutney sandwich?' Riley explained, grabbing her round her vast waist and trying, vainly, to hug her.

'I have to,' Flora said. 'Otherwise Riley lies in wait for them. He fries them. In slices.'

'Lovely with lots of salt,' said Riley, merrily smacking his lips. 'Tasty. Yum-yum!'

The leopard's cage was filled with suitcases and battered trunks. A number of boxes labelled:

FOOD FOR THOUGHT
VEGETARIAN RESTAURANT
GIBBET FIELD
BUCKINGHAM

were stacked in a lop-sided pyramid along one wall.

'All our equipment's packed in there,' Riley said mournfully. 'I hope it isn't rusting.'

'Don't *worry* so,' Flora rebuked him, moving on hastily to yet another cage.

This one had such a cosy lived-in look that Ally was astonished. The walls were hung with bright materials, the bars draped with a patchwork screen of gaily coloured rugs pinned over one another to keep out wind and weather.

The floor was cluttered with yet more rugs, and woven baskets piled with fruit and pamphlets, and bunches of dried herbs.

'Flora made all of these,' said Riley, pointing indiscriminately around the cage at rugs and clothes, materials and baskets. 'A few of her many self-survival skills from earlier, halcyon days, when this whole nutty venture was still a twinkle in her eye.'

'They make it all look very comfy,' Ally said. He was quite envious. He wouldn't mind living in here with Flora.

'It all just keeps us mouldering down here that much longer,' Riley responded sourly.

Ally looked down. 'Who's this, then?'

Inside a shallow basket at his feet there lay a mother cat. Her tail had spilled untidily over the edge and each time it flicked, three tawny kittens charged and battered it in flurried rushes.

'That's Saffron,' said Flora with a smile. 'We've been together years. She's such a friendly cat.'

'I'm fond of Saffron, too,' Riley agreed surprisingly, adding, to spoil it, 'Some nights, she helps me on my hunting trips. We shared a splendid *Vole Mornay* last week, didn't we, Saffron?'

Flora looked coldly at him.

'What about these?' asked Ally, bending to poke the scrumming balls of fluff outside the mother's basket. 'What are their names?'

'Salsa, Sesame and Soy,' Flora named them all proudly. 'I'm going to raise them all as vegetarians.'

'A chilly day in hell before you do,' scoffed Riley. 'Soy had some of my sautéed bat last night and licked his lips for hours. I've promised him a nice *Batatouille* some time.'

Flora had had enough. She flounced out, her lovely eyes flashing with rage.

Ally gazed after her mournfully. Had the one spoonful of the soup he'd swallowed not still been lying deep in his stomach, a small gob of unease, he might have changed his mind right there and then about giving her up, she looked so beautiful.

He turned to Riley. 'What's that fantastic stuff she rubs around her eyes?'

'Kohl,' Riley said.

'Coal?' Ally checked again, aghast and stunned. '*Coal?*'

'Yes, kohl,' said Riley, getting irritable. 'Haven't you ever heard of kohl before?'

'Of *course* I've heard of coal,' Ally snapped back. '*Everyone* has.'

They shouldered one another, snarling, out of the cage.

Chapter 17

Flora and Ally sat on the grass, watching Aunt Chloe wander around the clearing admiring the butterflies.

'She looks quite happy,' Flora said. 'When you consider . . .'

'I think it's something about being down here,' Ally explained. 'Up on the hill, she sits all hunched inside herself and saying nothing, as if she's terrified that everything around her might explode at any minute. This time she's been in hospital for seven whole weeks, and till today I didn't think that she was getting better.'

'She's certainly very taken with the butterflies.'

'She likes this place. And I think maybe that's because it's stopped being what it used to be, but isn't anything else yet. It's almost a place out of time. So she feels safe here.'

'It is very peaceful, isn't it?' Flora agreed. 'That's why I've been so stubborn about staying down here as long as I can. Riley's quite scathing about it. He keeps on muttering about "good vibes" not being quite as useful as proper medical care.'

'Well,' Ally said, 'you are still in the hospital grounds.'

'Not the right *sort* of hospital,' Flora reminded him. And then she sighed. Ally leaned back to stare at the sunlit sprinkles overhead. A tune that he'd been practising on his flute ran through his mind, and after a while he found that he was humming it aloud. After a few more moments he realized Flora knew the tune as well and had joined in.

He hadn't known the melody had words. He lay and listened as the song floated across the clearing.

' *"If I'd been told of the dangers of falling*
 I would have stayed safely down on my
  knees;
 If I'd been warned of the chances of tripping

I wouldn't have danced in the soft summer breeze.
All time's a journey to risks and disasters,
Triumphs and passions, lost loves, parted ways.
Stay on the safe side. Or move to the other
And fill your whole life with kaleidoscope days."'

The song came to an end, but Ally just lay happily. The words made good sense, he thought. Not being frightened of what might happen tomorrow. Not being scared to live.

'I think that Chloe ought to pay attention to that song,' he said at last. 'I think that she should try to toughen up. Face a few worries. Try to be happier.'

Flora rolled over to look at him. 'You're a sweet boy,' she told him. 'You're good with people. There should be more like you about, and then Aunt Chloe wouldn't feel the need to hide away.'

The admiration was sincere. The smudged eyes shone. And Ally fell in love all over again.

He didn't get the chance to make the most of it. Almost at once, Riley was at their side. 'Your aunt's in a good mood,' he said to Ally. 'Humming away over there.'

'Aunt Chloe used to sing,' said Ally. 'She's quite musical. She plays the flute as well.' He scowled. 'Except she stopped when she got ill again, and Mum has borrowed it to make me take lessons, just so it isn't wasted.'

'That's *terrible*,' said Flora. 'I didn't think people did things as cruel as that these days.'

He looked at her through narrowed eyes. Could she be teasing?

'It doesn't matter,' he said stalwartly. 'It won't be for much longer. I'm sure Aunt Chloe will soon be out of hospital. And even if she has to go back any time, Mum will make her take the flute with her because they're going to start an orchestra up on the hill as soon as they can find the time to get it going.'

'Really?' said Flora. 'An orchestra? Up on the hill?'

'There are a lot of people up there,' Ally said. 'You'd be surprised. In fact, there should be more. But they're so short-staffed, being stuck out here, they can't take all the patients that they should. But even so they've got enough to start an orchestra. And that's just people who know how to play already. There are some others who'd quite like to learn. Nurse Beddowes told me she's been saving up for months and months to buy a harp.'

'Heavens!' said Riley reverently.

'I wish they'd get a move on,' Ally said. His voice was wistful. 'They've had this plan for *months*. The only thing holding them up is that all the staff are so busy.' He kicked a clod of earth from one foot to another. 'I'd help them if they'd let me. Really I would.'

'I bet you would,' said Riley.

'What they need up there,' Flora said thoughtfully, 'is a good manager.'

A strange glint shone in her eyes.

'Flora's a manager,' Riley explained. 'She used to manage me, didn't you, Flora, *mein Führer, mein Kamp Kommandant*? She's managed lots of things. A yoga centre. Then a weaving workshop with a basket-making annexe. And, after that, a vegetarian restaurant called *Food for Thought*. That's where we met. She managed me into a job and then, after a short sharp quarrel over bacon bits, managed me out of it.'

'What job?' asked Ally rather suspiciously. He found it hard to think of Riley working with Flora, and not just hindering her.

'I am a cook,' said Riley with some pride. 'A very good one, too, with something of a reputation among all the gourmands of Gibbet Field, Buckingham.'

'Yes,' Flora said archly. 'A reputation for putting bacon bits into the vegetarian soup.'

Better than mouse turds, Ally thought privately.

'If you're a cook,' he said to Riley, still suspiciously, 'why didn't you cook lunch?'

Riley's eyes strayed across the clearing and came to rest on Flora's makeshift stove.

'I said I was a *cook*,' he told him frostily. 'I didn't say I was a *witch*.'

Ally lowered his head to hide his smile. He didn't want to hurt Flora's feelings, but it was very funny all the same.

And Flora seemed to think so too. She made a little choking noise that Ally heard as laughter.

'Oh, no!' said Riley, reaching out for her. 'Oh, no! Oh, not yet, *please*, Flora my love!'

Chapter 18

Nervously, Ally scrambled to his feet.

Aunt Chloe hurried back across the clearing and stood beside him, watching Flora.

'There, there,' she muttered soothingly, and leaned down to lay a hand on the bright, distended skirt. 'There, there, Flora.'

Aunt Chloe looked quite different, Ally thought. For one thing, she was smiling. Her peaky face had softened, making her look a whole lot younger. Perhaps, he thought, that dreadful soup of Flora's had somehow done her good. Her skin looked pinker and fresher, and her pale eyes shone.

Flora let out her breath again as the cramp passed.

Aunt Chloe's smile grew more intense. She

looked quite radiant. 'There, there,' she said again, still patting comfortingly. 'There, there, Flora.'

Riley stretched down a hand to Flora. 'Come on, my own sweet artichoke heart. Our days in the wilderness are over. Time to rejoin the world.'

Flora drew back. 'Not yet, Riley. Don't be silly. Babies take *ages*.'

Indeed the spasm did seem to have passed, and she looked quite herself again, and in control.

'That's fine,' said Riley. 'I don't mind how long the baby takes. I just want to be near some help.'

'Quite right,' said Ally. (Just the sight of Flora doubled over with that cramp had put him in a fright.)

'Riley,' said Flora, 'don't start to fuss at me now. There's nothing wrong, and I don't want anyone "helping me" until it's time. I've managed beautifully so far. I'll manage this. So don't go *panicking*. Everything's under control.'

Ally pitched in on Riley's side. 'Flora—'

'No!' she insisted in a tone more terse than she had ever used to him before. 'I'll *manage*, Ally. I don't want to be bossed around, and poked and prodded at for hours, and told what I'm to do, and have this time all spoiled for me. I'm staying here in peace for just a little longer. I will *manage* it.'

'This is a *baby*, not a restaurant,' Riley insisted. He turned to Ally. 'Have you got a phone?'

Poor Ally could have kicked himself for letting his morning burst of petulant independence rob him of something so useful. He shook his head.

Riley gnawed at his fingers. 'She should be near professional help. Something might go all wrong.'

'Stop *worrying*, Riley!' Flora shrieked at him.

Ally could see that yet another cramp was washing over her, making her ratty. But to his horror, Riley turned away, biting his lip.

'Listen,' Ally suggested eagerly. 'Why don't I just run up to the hospital and try to find Nurse Beddowes or one of the doctors? I won't tell them that there's anyone down here. I'll just ask for advice.'

'No!' Flora snapped. 'It'll be hours yet. First babies can take *days*.'

'And they can come in no time at all, as well,' said Riley. '*Please*, Flora? You've never had a child before so you don't know.'

'Riley's right,' Ally said. 'I'd really better run up there and get some help.'

He was astonished when she turned on him. Her eyes flashed. Tangled hair fell round her pale strained face. Still bent with cramp, she shook her finger at him like a witch. 'You promised me you'd never, *ever* tell. That's what you said. I'm holding you to that, Alasdair Seton. So if you break your word and tell anyone up on that hill that Riley and I are down here before I'm ready, I'll never speak to you again.'

It really sounded like a curse this time. And, swinging round, she added: 'That goes for you too, Riley!'

Riley went white.

'She doesn't mean it,' Ally said, tugging at Riley's sleeve. 'And even if she does, you mustn't *let* her.'

'I've warned you, *both* of you,' Flora repeated, still doubled over, clutching at her skirt.

'She means it,' Riley said in a pathetic tone of voice that Ally never had imagined he'd hear him use. 'She always does. She said she'd sack me over those bacon bits, even without another cook to take my place, even if it meant packing in the restaurant she'd worked so hard to start. And sure enough, she did it.'

Exasperated, Ally howled, 'Riley, for heaven's sake! That was just *silly*. Bacon bits! This is *important*!'

'So were the bacon bits for *me*, Ally,' Flora burst out defiantly, even though Ally could see it cost considerable effort.

'Riley,' wailed Ally. 'Stop this *dithering*. You've got to get Flora out of here. Just in case.'

But Riley wouldn't meet his eye. He sagged as if the stuffing had come out of him. His eyes glittered with tears. 'I can't,' he said. His voice was hoarse. 'I can't, in case she means it.'

Aunt Chloe suddenly stretched out her other hand and patted Riley on the arm. 'There, there,' she soothed him too. 'There, there, Riley.'

And Ally realized at last, looking at each of them in turn, that they were hopeless. It was up to him.

'Come on, Aunt Chloe,' he said impatiently. 'Quickly! Come on!'

He prised her hand away from Riley's arm and dragged her off, unwillingly, towards the wrought-iron gates.

Just as he pulled her through, she snatched her hand back, breaking away as she had done before on the old bridge, and started scurrying back towards Flora and Riley.

'Come here!' he yelled at her, angry and panicking. 'Come *back*, Aunt Chloe.'

She stopped and turned. Her face had the same stubborn look he'd seen the day she broke away from the nurse and waved across the tea room.

She shook her head.

'Oh, *stay* then,' Ally muttered, furious. 'You'd only slow me up in any case. You're never any use!'

He slipped between the slim, high, patterned gates and ran out, down the narrow twisting path that led back to the bridge.

Chapter 19

He hurried past the glass front of the office. The porter raised his head, gave him a curious stare and said through his small window:

'You're back at last then, are you?'

But Ally didn't have the time to stop and explain. Pretending he hadn't heard, he rushed on, pushing through the swing doors as quickly as he could.

He crossed the hall and hurried into the lift. As he turned round to watch the doors close, he saw his squelching shoes had left fat muddy splodges over the tiles.

'Sorry,' he called across, too late, as the doors closed. On the way up in the lift, he tried to think. He might find someone who could help.

But how would he get whoever it was down to the stone menagerie without mentioning Flora? And if he explained, then Flora's curse would come down on his head.

He didn't *believe* in curses. (After all, he wasn't *daft*.) But Flora had definitely meant what she said. Riley knew. Look at him! He had known Flora far, far longer than Ally had, and he had taken her threat so seriously he'd acted almost paralysed. He couldn't do the sensible thing.

Ally so wanted to keep the two of them as friends. He thought of doing nothing after all – just mooching round, pretending to himself that he was looking for a doctor or a nurse, but really wasting time. After all, Riley was obviously trusting to luck and trying to convince himself Flora was right and the birth of the baby was still several hours away.

But Riley had much more to lose if Flora kept her word and never spoke to him again. Look at the way he'd crumpled when she just threatened it. He'd obviously tried to convince himself that, since she was such a brilliant manager, she was managing this.

But Ally wasn't quite so sure. Those cramps had doubled Flora over every time. Didn't that mean that things were moving fast? And how would he ever feel at ease in Flora's company again, knowing he'd taken such a risk?

He wouldn't. It would spoil everything.

Perhaps he could get one of the doctors down there without explaining.

No. That was a daft idea. They were already run off their feet. They wouldn't go off traipsing through weeds and over backwaters and into woods simply because he said there *was* a reason, really, down at the other end, but he could not explain it.

He had no choice. He had to find somebody sensible and tell them Flora's secret. Flora might change her mind, lift the curse and forgive him – though Riley hadn't held out too much hope for that, what with the bacon bits.

And if she didn't?

Well, he'd be lonely once again. He'd lose a friend. Two, if you counted Riley. At least he'd know he'd done his best to act responsibly. And knowing that might be some consolation in all the quarrels to come about the sort of things that he would eat, and entertainments where he thought animals might be unhappy, and all that other stuff he could see coming when he and his parents wouldn't see eye to eye, but he was just expected to back down as he had always done before, but wouldn't any longer.

He'd feel more armed, as if he'd come through some initiation rite.

Sadder and stronger, like Sir Lancelot.

Cheered by this image, Ally stepped out bravely through the opening lift doors into the corridor. It was a short walk along to Dr Barney's office. He tapped, then, hearing her voice, he took a deep breath for courage and went in.

The room took Ally by surprise. He had assumed that it would look like his own doctor's office – clean and bright, with a computer on a desk, one or two shiny trolleys loaded with strange equipment, and a high bed with plastic curtains that could be pulled across.

This was an old-fashioned room with faded carpet and dark shelves of blackened wood. Instead of a desk, there was a massive table with a leather top and fluted legs. Behind that was a huge carved fireplace. Heavy red curtains framed the giant windows, and on the walls hung old-fashioned pictures in fancy frames.

For just a moment, Dr Barney kept on writing. Ally stayed quiet as he gazed around. Over the mantelpiece there was a faded print in a curious filigree frame of tarnished metal coiled into serpents, just like the wrought iron gates that led into the stone menagerie.

The very same pattern, Ally was sure of it. The very same.

In fact, now he came to look more closely, surely he could see—

Just at that moment Dr Barney lifted her head.

'Ah, good!' she said. 'You're back! Nurse Beddowes had become quite anxious about the two of you staying away so long and missing lunch. She's telephoned all round the hospital several times, trying to find you. Chloe's gone off, I suppose, to have her supper?'

Supper? Was it that late? It couldn't be! He'd made a point of telling his mother that he'd be home on time. She would be furious. *And* sick with worry.

But it was important not to think about that now. He had to get some help to Flora.

Dr Barney frowned, and it was obvious to Ally that she was thinking he had already wasted enough of everyone else's time in one way or another, not letting people know when he'd be back. And now he was standing like a simpleton, wasting hers.

'She *has* gone off to supper, hasn't she?' she asked more sharply.

'No,' Ally said, after a pause.

'She did come back with you, didn't she?'

'No,' Ally said again. 'She wouldn't come.'

He didn't say any more. An idea that might get him off the hook with Flora, and yet get somebody sensible down to the clearing, was hatching in his mind.

He looked up. Dr Barney was staring at him, horrified.

'She wouldn't *come*?'

'No.'

He took the plunge. It was, he realized, rather a desperate measure. It might not even work. But never mind. He'd try it anyway, and then be even more responsible next time he had the chance, to square things up.

'No,' he repeated, slowly and clearly. 'I tried to bring her, but she wouldn't come.'

Chapter 20

He pointed above the fireplace. 'Look on the map.'

'What map?'

It was quite clear that, all the time she'd had this room, she'd never bothered to inspect the print inside the frame. But from the moment he had spotted that same distinctive pattern as on the old menagerie gates, Ally had been looking more carefully. He had already guessed that it was one of those old picture maps – the sort he'd seen in comics. Usually they showed a desert island strewn with palms. There'd be a couple of spades leaning against one another in the sand, and heaps of sun-bleached bones. On a small hill would flutter a tattered skull-and-crossbones flag, and to the side, drawn shipwrecked on some vicious reef, a weed-strewn galleon.

'Hundreds of prizes to be won!' it might say underneath. 'Put in an X to mark the spot where you think Captain Bloodthroat buried his treasure.'

This map was far less crude. It showed the house and grounds as they had been a long, long time ago, before the seventh earl ran out of money and had to sell his home.

'See?' Ally said.

He laid a finger on the glass. The map behind had faded to the palest brown. There was a blotty stain up in the corner where all the sheds and the new kitchen block would have been drawn if they'd been built then.

'That's where we are.'

The hospital itself was drawn as the handsome house that it must once have been, complete with all its original pillars and porticoes. It stood against a ribbon of trees that must have been cut down a good few years before to clear a space for the car park.

'See? Here's the drive.'

The sweep of it was just the same. But to the

sides, where there was flat lawn now, Ally saw rose gardens and arbours, and trellised walks.

Now Dr Barney was peering closely too. 'Is that a *maze*?'

He realized she was right. In front of a line of pointy-roofed greenhouses connected by tiled paths, there was a little maze made out of privet hedges.

The patients would have liked that, Ally thought. It was a shame that it was gone.

A tiny carriage was being drawn by two fat-bellied horses up to an old front door that had since been replaced by new swing doors. He couldn't think how anyone could manage to draw things so delicately and so small. The shadow of his finger fell on two tiny men encouraging a flock of miniature sheep through a small wicket gate.

He slid his finger down the glass. 'We went down here.' he said. 'Towards the water.'

The lake looked different on the map – a fatter, tidier shape. The map-maker had put in water-lilies, smaller than poppy seeds. But they were all at one end of the lake, grown in a half-moon curve. They've spread and spread, he told himself.

Now the whole lake is choked to the very middle.

He slid his finger to the side, where the back-water flowed in. 'We were down here,' said Ally.

Above his finger was a pleasure pool dotted with boats in which elegant ladies clutching their parasols lay quite at ease, punted by slim tall men. A line of stone could be seen where Ally had crossed the stagnant water, soaking his shoes, but curving over it was drawn a real arched bridge with fancy curving parapets, and ladies in long dresses leaning over to wave to friends in boats.

'The bridge is gone,' he said to Dr Barney. 'But see that stone ridge underneath? Well, that's still there, and that's how we got across the water.'

He didn't say another word. He let his eyes move down to where the tiny gates to the menagerie were drawn. Behind them were the squat cages in a ring, and men and women walking arm in arm around the clearing followed by prancing children, all pointing and laughing at the animals that glowered back at them.

Riley was right, he saw. The pit had bears. A great tall post, like a drab maypole, stood in the centre for the bears to climb. That wasn't down there now unless it lay, covered in undergrowth, somewhere outside the clearing. The tiger paced in that same cage Riley had guessed for him. The monkeys hung in writhing, desperate clusters along their bars. The elephant stood stamping, tethered and cramped.

He saw Dr Barney's finger slide down the glass until it reached the part of the print that showed the water.

'You left her *here*? Ally, you're seriously telling me you left Chloe all *alone*? Down by the *lake*?'

Oh, he knew perfectly well why she was so appalled. He knew that she was thinking about the scars on Chloe's wrists, and how someone like her shouldn't be left all by herself down by a reedy lake.

She didn't know that Chloe was happier than she'd been for weeks. And there was someone else to worry about much more today.

Keeping his eye on the menagerie to make less of a lie of what he was about to say, Ally told Dr Barney firmly, 'Yes. That's where I left her. That's where she is.'

For just a moment, Dr Barney didn't speak. She stood a little longer, staring at the map, that anxious, puzzled frown still on her face. Then, reaching for a leather bag with thick brass clasps, she led him from the hospital the quickest way, through corridors he'd never seen, and down an unmarked lift, out through a side door.

On the wide lawns she slowed her steps, uncertain, the old brown map already hazy in her mind.

'This way,' said Ally, stepping in front of her. 'We go down here. Mind all the brambles.'

Chapter 21

Riley was sitting on the far side of the swamp, his knees drawn up, a smile upon his face, gazing down into the water. His clothes were dappled in rosy patches from the evening sunlight filtering through the leaves. His face was the same pink, but pink all over.

Hearing the grasses rustle as they approached, he leaped to his feet. 'There you are, Ally!'

In his excitement he jumped up and down, bursting with happiness.

Both of his shoes fell off into the swamp.

'Oh, damn it!' he cried, fishing among the reeds to catch them for the second time that day. 'Damn it.'

'That's Riley, that is,' Ally whispered.

'Riley . . . ?'

Hoping she wouldn't press him for an explanation till they had got to Flora, Ally knelt down, pretending not to hear, and tugged at his laces. His shoes had not yet dried from his last hurried crossing. The drier they were when Ally's mother saw them, the less fuss there would be, and so he took them off again, and Dr Barney followed his example.

Riley, who'd salvaged both his shoes by now, scrambled back to his feet and yelled across.

'I had a girl! A baby girl! And she looks just like me!'

Dr Barney's eyes narrowed.

'Flora did, really,' Ally whispered. Then he stepped smartly out onto the slimy stonework, to save himself from Dr Barney's next question.

'So who is Flora?'

Riley stretched out a hand to each of them in turn as they reached the far bank.

'Are you a doctor?' he said, spotting the leather bag. 'Oh, that is splendid! I'm sure that Flora will take off the curse, now that the whole thing's over.'

'The curse?'

Her voice was casual, calm, professional. Only her steely eyes gave her away.

'Only on Ally,' Riley assured her comfortably. 'Not on you, or me, or good old Aunty Chloe. Chloe was a tremendous help. She sterilized both of her sneaker laces all by herself in Flora's cooking pot, then used them to tie the baby's cord.'

'Sterilized sneaker laces? *Chloe?*'

'Yes. Very thoughtful of her, Flora said, then made me lend her mine.' He smiled beguilingly. 'That's why my shoes fell off into the swamp.'

'Again!' chortled Ally. He hadn't realized how relieved he was. But now he heard his own laughter echoing round them, he knew how very anxious he had been.

But it was over now. Flora had managed. He didn't even mind the baby looking like Riley. He was just very glad things were all right. He'd face the row for being so late home quite calmly now.

'She needed laces more than I did, I suppose,' Riley was saying dubiously, rather as if, stuck in his dripping socks, he still needed convincing. 'She would keep rushing to and fro, finding a nice woollen rug to wrap it in, and walking it up and down the cage, and crooning to it.'

He saw the baffled faces.

'The baby, that is. Not the nice woollen rug.'

'Baby? Aunt Chloe?'

The tone that Dr Barney used was non-committal. Her eyes told another story.

But Riley had turned back to Ally.

'She's good with babies, your Aunt Chloe is. She knows all those old lullabies, all about hush and sleepy-byes, droopy eyelids and such. She says she'll teach them all to both of us, and Flora's grateful because all she could think of was some song she said she'd sung to you but didn't want to sing to the baby till she was a good deal older. And all I could remember was the first verse of *Three Blind Mice*, which isn't suitable at all, and a short rousing anti-vivisection anthem we learned last Easter at the Swindon rally.'

'We should get on,' Ally broke in. He was quite terrified that Dr Barney might suddenly decide that Riley needed professional help and leap upon him with some huge syringe, to calm him down.

'Right-ho!' said Riley, reaching down to pick up

Dr Barney's bag. 'My, this is heavy. What have you got in here? Tinned meat, I hope, in glorious celebration!'

'Tinned meat?'

But as she stared, he skipped off through the overhanging greenery, leaving them both to catch up if they could.

'That's Riley,' Ally said again, feeling a word or two of explanation was called for, but mindful that, as yet, the curse still stood.

'Riley,' said Dr Barney, rather faintly. 'How very nice to meet him. And where are we going now?'

Chapter 22

Flora was sitting half propped up on a pile of rugs that had been covered with shawls and woven cloths, and Riley's old cooking aprons. She looked pale and excited, and very beautiful. She'd taken the baby back, wrapped in its rug, after persuading Chloe that Salsa and Sesame were needing cuddles too, after all the excitement.

The two small kittens scrapped in Chloe's lap while Soy raced around the floor, all over-wrought, chewing the ends of Riley's shoelaces in Aunty Chloe's sneakers.

Dr Barney stayed by the bars, staring in mute astonishment at this strange, makeshift home. But Riley strode across the cage. 'Flora, my mushroom, this is Dr Barney.'

'She didn't know about you,' Ally put in as quickly as he could. 'She came to fetch Aunt Chloe.'

Then he saw Chloe's anguished look and felt quite dreadful.

'I'll bring you down again, if we're allowed,' he told her, and added hopefully, 'If Dr Barney lets us come, and Flora wants us back.'

Aunt Chloe gave a tiny stricken shrug, and turned for comfort to the lolling kittens.

'How are you, Chloe?' Dr Barney said. The small unusual signs of attention hadn't escaped her.

Aunt Chloe gave a nod, scarcely perceptible. Her head hung down.

Ally decided that he'd deserted his aunt for long enough. He wasn't going to fail to support her now.

'She's had a really good day,' he said enthusiastically. 'Aunt Chloe's enjoyed herself a lot. She has been humming to herself and walking round looking at butterflies. And magpies.'

Remembering he'd made the magpie up, he blushed and pressed on fast.

'She ate a good lunch.' Asking for more of

Flora's soup was not, in Ally's view, the sign of a return to mental health, but Dr Barney wouldn't realize that. '*And* she had seconds. She never started blinking once. I even think she listened some of the time, because she giggled when I made a joke. *And* she spoke once or twice.'

Twisting his fingers round, he added nervously in case it sounded ungrateful, 'I think she likes it much better down here than in the hospital. That's why she didn't want to go back.'

'Talking of *hospitals*, Flora, my walnut kernel, my sweet dried apricot . . .' Riley began to wheedle.

'Oh, very well,' said Flora. 'Just for a very short visit. Just for a checkup.' She beamed triumphantly and hugged the wrapped-up baby even closer. 'Since it's all over, and everyone agrees that even though I wasn't right about how long it would take, still I did *manage*.'

'You did, you *did*,' crowed Riley ecstatically. 'You managed *beautifully*. You always do.' He prised the ruggy baby out of her arms, took one more long admiring look, then gave it back to her. 'But now it's quite important to let Dr Barney take a tiny peep at you, then get you somewhere clean and nice, so they can make sure everything is tickety-boo.'

'Oh, all right,' Flora said. 'I must say, I could do with spending a night in a proper bed. I am *exhausted*.'

'I cannot tell you how irregular I find all this,' said Dr Barney.

'Syrup of figs,' said Flora absently, poking inside the rug.

'Right, then,' said Riley. 'Everyone out! The quicker we get this show on the road, the quicker I get within snatching distance of a bacon sandwich.' He rushed around the cage, finding another shawl to wrap round Flora's shoulders to keep her warm on the way through the woods.

Flora called Ally back, just for a moment.

'The curse is off,' she whispered in his ear. 'I'm glad you're back.'

He smiled and, on an impulse, stuck out a finger to push the tiny golden bells in her ears and hear them jangle once again. It was the closest thing to kissing her that he dared do, and even so it made him blush.

He stumbled out, leaving the mother and her baby with Dr Barney in the cosy cage.

Chapter 23

'Call it a madman's opinion if you will,' Riley was saying airily, a short time later, sprawled on the grass. 'I cannot see the harm in spraying greenfly.'

'Riley!' came Flora's voice across the darkening clearing.

'Oh, God! She *heard*!' said Riley, affecting terror. 'Defend me, Ally! Back me up! I did drink all your soup.'

'*Riley!*'

Flora was standing rather unsteadily outside the cage at Dr Barney's side. Behind her, Aunt Chloe was carrying the baby.

'We're going now,' Flora announced. 'I'm fit to walk as far as the bridge so long as I take it slowly.

And the sooner we're out of here the better. Dr Barney is worried that Sanity might get a chill in these dank, miserable cages.'

'Dank, miserable cages?' Riley echoed open-mouthed. '*Sanity?*'

Flora came over, resting on Dr Barney's arm. 'I thought we'd call the baby Sanity, Riley. It sounds such a nice name.'

'Don't be *ridiculous*,' snapped Riley. 'You can't call her that. You give a child a potty name like Sanity and after one false move—' He dropped his voice to hushed and threatening tones. 'One *tiny* false move, Flora my lettuce leaf, like simply boy-cotting the nursery school's annual day trip to the zoo, and council busybodies will be queuing up to rip the child out of your arms and take it into care. Right, Dr Barney?'

'Well . . .' Dr Barney began.

'*Right!*' Ally said. Sanity was an *awful* name. He'd back Riley up to the hilt on that, soup or no soup.

'Perhaps you're right,' said Flora anxiously. 'I don't think Dr Barney cared for the idea, either. Did you?'

'No,' Dr Barney said. 'Frankly, I didn't.'

'There,' Riley said. 'See?'

'What's *your* name, then?' Flora asked Dr Barney in just that tone of voice Ally remembered with a pang she'd used on him the day she was considering planting his name.

'Elizabeth,' Dr Barney said. 'Elizabeth Mary Barney.'

She sounded rather pleased for the first time that day.

'*Lovely*,' said Riley, snapping up this suggestion as quickly as possible, hoping to forestall worse. 'That settles it. Elizabeth.'

'*Chloe* Elizabeth,' Ally suggested suddenly, and everyone stared.

'Chloe Elizabeth . . .'

Flora tried out the name, softly, as Ally had tried out hers the first time he saw it from the high tea-room window.

Everyone turned to look at Aunt Chloe, to see how she would take to the idea. A pale pink glow came to her cheeks. She hugged the baby tighter.

'Yes,' Riley said. 'Chloe Elizabeth.'

He prised the ruggy baby out of Aunt Chloe's arms. 'Come on then, Chloe Elizabeth,' he said. 'Let's get you safely out of this horrid, nasty, damp old clearing, before you rust like all my cooking things, and it gets dark, and Ally's parents storm the hospital and drag the lake for all our missing bodies.' He turned to Flora. 'You're sure you can get as far as the bridge?'

'I'm tired and sore,' Flora informed Riley tartly. 'I am not *lame*.'

Resting on Riley's arm, she set off gingerly towards the gates. Just as they reached them, Riley spun round and winked at Chloe. As though some cunning plan was pre-arranged, she promptly turned and scuttled back into the cage. Then, moments later, she came out again, carrying a large woven basket covered with a patchwork shawl. And as she hurried after Flora, Ally could not help but notice a trail of torn pamphlets floating after her out of the basket, as if they might be being patted out by cross little paws.

Turning again to check on his little procession, Riley caught sight of Dr Barney's baffled face.

'You mustn't worry,' he said cheerfully. 'Everything will turn out fine. Flora will manage beautifully. She always does. Doesn't she, Ally?'

'Yes,' Ally said. 'She does.'

'See?' Riley chortled. 'This way. Mind all the brambles, everyone.'

Ally looked around the clearing one last time, then back towards the gates. Already the others were disappearing down the narrow path between the trees. He felt exhausted suddenly. What were the last words of the song Flora had sung only a couple of hours before? *Fill your whole life with kaleidoscope days*.

Well, this had certainly been one. And there would be the big rehearsal tomorrow. That would be another.

But right now he simply wanted to go home. He didn't care that there would be a giant row before he was allowed to vanish upstairs to bed.

Ally just wanted to be back.

'Wait for me, Aunty Chloe,' he called suddenly. 'Please! Wait for me!'

She heard. Resting the basket on the grass, she even turned and waited, till he caught up.

Chapter 24

Nurse Beddowes stood, hands on hips, defending Crispin Hospital single-mindedly from Flora's strained look and Riley's blandishments.

'This is a psychiatric hospital,' she repeated stonily. 'So we don't have any infant or maternity beds.'

'That's all right,' Riley coaxed. 'Flora's not choosy, are you, my sprouting lentil? We'll take any old bed, won't we, my blossom? And failing that, a stable. Some old manger . . .'

'You can't have one of our beds,' Nurse Beddowes said. 'Go to the General Hospital out on the Munford by-pass. They have all sorts of beds there. Our beds are psychiatric.'

'Really?' said Riley. 'Psychiatric beds? Which would you like to sleep in, Flora, my love? A breakdown bed that shakes a bit? A paranoid bed behind concealing curtains? A psychopathic bed whose mattress might rear up and smother you in the night on sudden vicious impulse? Or twin schizophrenic beds? That's all they have. They don't have any stable, feet-on-the-ground maternity beds. Their beds are psychiatric.'

'That isn't funny,' Dr Barney said, trying hard not to laugh.

'She means the patients, not the beds,' Ally explained to Riley.

'He knows exactly what I mean,' Nurse Beddowes said sourly.

'It's most short-sighted of you,' Riley persisted. 'I thought the National Health Service believed in prophylaxis nowadays.'

'Prophy *what*?' Ally said.

'Prophylaxis,' Riley repeated for him patiently. 'Stopping the rot before it starts. And any child brought up by Flora here is bound to come back some time, after all.'

'Oh,' Ally said, startled. But then he realized it was just another ploy. Riley could not be serious.

Flora, thought Ally, would be a wonderful mother. And Chloe Elizabeth might not realize it for quite some time, but she was very lucky.

Nurse Beddowes was still fighting back. 'We can't afford to think about things that way. We're too short-staffed.'

'How about giving us jobs, then?' Riley suggested promptly. 'You could employ us both. Me from tomorrow, and Flora bit by bit, after a few days' rest. And you could rent us one of those empty staff flats above the old coach house.'

All the time he was talking, he kept a hand behind his back and made little stabbing motions with his finger towards the floor under Aunt Chloe's chair. Ally looked down, then hastily dropped to his knees as if to re-knot his laces while surreptitiously he pushed the struggling kittens back into the basket. He tucked the coverlet more firmly round them and their mother before Nurse Beddowes noticed them and had a fit.

'Give you both jobs?' Nurse Beddowes eyed Riley with the deepest suspicion. 'What do you do, anyway?'

'Flora here is a basket maker of some note,'

Riley said proudly. 'One of her finest is lying under Chloe's chair right now. No! Don't slide it out, Aunt Chloe! Show it to Nurse Beddowes *later*, when things are *settled*! And Flora weaves, and prints on cloth beautifully too. That shawl she's wearing is her own work entirely. And she wove this nice woollen rug in which the baby's wrapped.'

He pointed, prodded, felt the cloth, waved at the basket under Aunt Chloe's chair, and Ally realized that he must be desperate to find them a home, to sell their wares so forcefully.

'There *must* be some small niche for her in Occupational Therapy, if you're short-staffed,' Riley insisted. 'And I myself, as an experienced cook, am quite as capable of slicing Spam as the next kitchen lady.'

'Riley!' said Flora, looking up, shocked. '*Spam?* Have you no scruples?'

'Scruples?' He dropped on his knees beside her, urgent, appealing. 'Scruples, my parsley sprig? There was a time for scruples once, I agree. And there will be again, I promise you. Soon. But right now we're penniless and homeless with a baby to support. We have to bend a little, Flora, just to survive. Life is a subtle business.' He took her hand and squeezed it tenderly. 'And I won't even lick my fingers after I've sliced the ham, I promise you. I'll wipe them on my apron.'

Nurse Beddowes, moved by this little speech, smiled fondly at him. It was her first nice look since he came in.

Flora sighed heavily, peeping inside the rug.

'Maybe you're right,' she said. 'I do feel very tired. A cosy warm staff flat would be so nice. And if I had a job here, I could weave again, couldn't I?'

'You could weave bonnets for Chloe Elizabeth before the nasty weather comes,' Riley wheedled shamelessly. 'And baskets for her to sleep in.'

'Like Moses,' Ally said.

'How can she work?' Nurse Beddowes appealed to Dr Barney, arms thrown wide. 'She has a new-born *baby*. It's most irregular.'

'Bran,' Flora muttered automatically. 'Failing that, senna pods.'

Nurse Beddowes stared at her.

'I'm sure she'll manage,' Dr Barney said. 'It seems she always does.'

'Aunt Chloe could help out,' suggested Ally.

'With all the cuddling and lullabies and stuff like that.' An optimistic thought struck. 'While she's still with you, that is. And after, when she's well enough to leave, she could still come and help Flora. The baby is named after her, after all, so she's halfway to being family.'

He knew he was pushing his luck in his attempt to convince Nurse Beddowes everything would work out well. But good things could happen. So why shouldn't this?

Filled with enthusiasm, he carried on. 'After all, singing and cuddling the baby was what Aunt Chloe wanted to do anyway. Those kittens in that basket there are only second-best.'

Realizing what he'd said, he clapped his hand over his mouth.

It was too late.

'Kittens?' Nurse Beddowes screeched. '*Kittens?* Have you brought kittens onto my ward? My patients will get worms!'

Chapter 25

'Worms?' Flora, defeated, turned to Dr Barney. 'Worms?'

'There!' Dr Barney said triumphantly. 'You've been trumped, Flora. My own profession, humble as it is in your eyes, still has some role to play where herbal healing has its limitations. You can't treat worms. I can.'

'Really?' said Riley, fascinated. 'You can treat worms? It staggers me you'd ever notice they were sick.'

'She means treat patients who have worms, not treat the worms themselves,' Ally explained.

'He knows exactly what she means,' Nurse Beddowes chimed in again, but not as sourly as before. She turned to Riley. 'What about references?' she asked. 'The hospital makes these decisions, not the nursing staff or any of the doctors. And they won't take you on without a reference.'

'I have a splendid reference,' Riley boasted happily. 'The manager of *Food for Thought* Vegetarian Restaurant, Gibbet Field, Buckingham, wrote it for me the day I left. In it it says, amongst other things, that I am a cook of far more skill than probity.'

'I've never heard of Probity,' Nurse Beddowes argued suspiciously. 'And I watch all those cooking shows.'

'That's as may be,' said Riley. 'None the less, I have more skill. And when I left, the restaurant manager pressed on me a huge great tin of bacon bits to take away.'

Ally leaned over his knees to muffle his gasp of laughter.

'I have a reference too,' Flora declared. 'My last business partner wrote it. In it he says that he believes that I could manage anything on this earth I put my mind to managing. Then, in a short P.S., he says he thinks that he is probably seriously under-estimating my abilities, and

I could more than likely manage a moon probe, too.'

'You could, you *could*,' Riley insisted generously. 'Whoever it was who wrote you that nice reference wrote no more than the truth.'

'A moon probe's rather difficult to prove,' Ally said slyly. 'An *orchestra*, now . . .'

'Chicken feed!' Flora declared. 'Simplicity itself, Ally. I promise you I'd have that flute of Aunt Chloe's back in her own hands within a week.'

'She would, she *would*,' hooted Riley.

'I have no doubt of it,' Dr Barney said. 'None whatsoever.'

'There!' Riley triumphed. 'Another glowing reference for your files, Nurse Beddowes.'

'You *ought* to take them on,' Ally said suddenly. 'I'm sure they'd be so good – cheer people up a bit. They've cheered up my Aunt Chloe such a lot in just one day. I think that you'd be *daft* not to employ them.' He heard the word *daft* go ringing round the tea room, so added hastily in case he had annoyed her, 'Of course, that's only my opinion I'm offering.'

'Of course it is,' Flora said crisply. 'If it were

anybody else's, you probably wouldn't bother to offer it, would you?'

'No,' Ally said, confused. 'No. I suppose I wouldn't.'

'I would think your opinion is quite as good as anybody else's,' Flora went on. 'Except on things like general topology, or mountain goat breeding techniques, about which you may know nothing. Isn't that right, Ally?'

'Yes,' Ally said, still confused. 'Yes, I suppose it is.'

The idea was quite new to him. It sounded strange but comforting, and might be useful in the rows to come.

'About this staff flat, then,' Riley was saying.

All at once, without warning, Nurse Beddowes changed tack.

'The way I see it,' she began quite pleasantly, 'you two are both *unhinged.*'

'We don't use that word here,' she was reminded gently by Dr Barney. 'I'm well aware that you are overwrought, Nurse Beddowes. But we don't use that word here in this hospital. And anyway, we can't throw Flora out tonight. So what it boils down to is a staff flat tonight, on trust, and interviews first thing tomorrow.' She added innocently, 'Or we could find them beds on the Acute Admissions ward. That's where you're on duty tonight, isn't it, Nurse?'

Nurse Beddowes stared at Riley, horrified. Riley began to grin at her, rolling his eyes.

She looked down at the the kittens in the basket, chewing Aunt Chloe's chair legs and shredding flakes of pamphlet on the floor, and her lip trembled.

She looked at Flora, nursing the tiny baby.

'I think I should warn you I'm a strict vegetarian,' Flora said amiably.

'She preaches, too,' said Riley. 'All the time. Mostly about Compassion in World Farming. And Animal Rights.'

He watched Nurse Beddowes with a sympathy born of shared experience as she surrendered promptly and totally.

'Staff flat,' she said. 'Staff flat it is, or I'll be taking up a bed myself on my own ward.'

'Now that's not kind,' Riley reproved her.

Nurse Beddowes shrugged. Now that she'd given up battling, she turned all practical.

'You should be lying down,' she ordered Flora.

'Put your feet up at once. I'll go and sort things out for you. It's time you and the baby had some peace and quiet.'

She turned on Riley.

'As for *you*,' she threatened him, 'you'll have to have an interview tomorrow, as Dr Barney said. And I should smarten up for it, if I were you. This is a hospital. You must be clean. Look at your *shoes*! Look at your *socks*!'

Obediently, Riley plucked at his trousers, revealing hairy legs.

Nurse Beddowes shrieked.

'*Look* at you! You've got *tide-marks* round your ankles! *Cook*, did you say you were? You look more like a *beachcomber* to me!'

She spun round on her rubber heels and strode towards the wide swing doors.

Just as she pushed at one side, the other half flew open.

In marched Ally's mother.

Chapter 26

'Ally!' His mother bore down on him. 'Ally, where have you *been*? We've both been worried sick about you. Have you the least idea what *time* it is? You left your phone at home. You never took your bike lights. You said that you'd be back in time for supper. We've rung and rung, and no one seemed to know where you and Chloe had gone, or if you'd come back yet. And so we've had to drag out and drive all the way over here just to start looking for you! I'm very cross indeed!'

Ally stared at the floor. The summer storm, he realized with some relief, had broken at last. That thin ice he'd been skating on all week had finally cracked.

Before he could get out a single word in his defence, his mother had rounded on her sister.

'Chloe! They said that you were lost! Oh, what a mess! I knew that Ally should never have come here alone today. I *knew* it. I have been fretting myself silly about it all week. I knew that if I wasn't here to keep an eye on both of you, things would go wrong.'

So *that's* what was going on, thought Ally. She was still thinking of him as if he were little more than three years old. Oh, this was almost certainly going to be one short sharp skirmish in a battle that would last for years.

Riley stepped in.

'Nothing went wrong,' he said. 'Things did go *differently*, I'll grant you, Mrs Seton. But nothing went *wrong*. Maybe things didn't go *your* way exactly. But they went none the worse for that.'

Grateful but horrified, Ally held his breath, waiting for some fresh outburst from his mother to land on his defender. But stunned into silence by Riley's sheer effrontery, Mrs Seton simply stared.

Riley smiled at her pleasantly. Infuriated, she turned back to Ally.

'Your shoes are *soaking* wet. They're very probably ruined. Well, I'm not paying for another pair just because you've spoiled those. Your supper's just a dish of cinders, too, and that's your fault. Kidneys just *shrivel* up, you know. You can't keep kidneys waiting.'

She looked around her crossly. Everyone else stared back, except for Flora, who was shuddering at the mere thought of kidneys shrivelling. Into the silence, his footsteps squeaking down the tea-room floor, walked Ally's father.

'Ah, so you found them!'

She'd barely noticed that he'd finally caught up with her. She was still grilling Ally.

'Where have you *been*? Answer me, straight away! And what on earth is going on in here? What is this little private evening meeting all about? Who *are* these people?'

She paused in her tirade, just for a moment, simply to glare her way around the circle of faces again.

Her eyes came to rest on Flora. Although she didn't say the word aloud, her tightened lips sent the message clearly enough: *Unkempt!*

She turned to search her husband's face for the

meek acquiescence that he and Ally knew she wouldn't rest until she'd seen.

'Straight off a broomstick,' rubber-stamped James Seton's face, promptly, obediently. And yet the look deep in his eyes wasn't so critical. And when his wife turned back again, bolstered, assuaged, his weak face softened up at once and showed a hint of wistful admiration.

'Have we met?' Nancy Seton asked, knowing full well they hadn't. For Flora wasn't just anyone – not someone you'd forget.

'I'm Flora Henderson,' Flora said crisply. 'I shall be helping out in Occupational Therapy.'

'I'm William Riley,' Riley said. 'I'm joining the kitchen staff. And this,' he added proudly, pointing to Flora's bundle, 'is Chloe Elizabeth Henderson-Riley.' Seeing the look on Flora's face, he added hastily, 'Or Riley-Henderson – we haven't had the time to quarrel properly about the order of the names yet.'

Mrs Seton looked mystified. 'You're trying to tell me that you've named that *rug*?'

'No,' Flora corrected Ally's mother tartly. 'Not the rug. The baby who's inside it.'

'They are both Flora's,' Riley explained. 'The rug and the baby.'

'It must be very *tiny*,' Ally's mother said accusingly.

A new voice broke in suddenly, small but determined. And very rude.

'They don't make diamonds quite as big as they make bricks.'

Chapter 27

Everyone stared.

Aunt Chloe went back to looking at her feet. But somehow, knowing that even she could gather herself to make such an enormous effort gave Ally courage.

'Listen,' he told his mother. 'I'm sorry. It was silly and irresponsible of me to leave the bike lights and the phone. But then the day went by so fast, I didn't realize what the time was until it was too late. But I am sorry.'

His mother met his apology with a raised eyebrow, and then repeated irritably, 'Your kidneys won't be fit to eat.'

Flora caught Ally's eye.

Knowing what she expected, he tried to look

away. But she had widened those huge blue eyes of hers, and tipped her head enquiringly. How could he let her down?

He sighed. He would have much preferred to leave this to some other time. Tell his plans to his mother another day.

Maybe tomorrow.

But then he thought: Perhaps Flora is right. Perhaps I shouldn't put it off. And I did tell Aunty Chloe that I was robust enough to handle things. I should see if it's true.

'I won't be eating kidneys any more,' Ally announced. 'I have become a vegetarian.'

Chloe looked up.

'A vegetarian?' His father was stunned.

'Good for you, Ally!' Riley declared cheerfully. 'And good luck, too!'

'Well, well, well,' murmured Dr Barney.

Flora smiled at him proudly, such a lovely smile. And that, alone, made it worth while.

His mother pursed her lips.

'We'll see,' she said in prim, clipped tones.

Tossing her head, she turned her back on him and made for the door, followed by Ally's father.

'A vegetarian indeed,' everyone heard her muttering. 'Well, we'll see about that.'

Ally supposed they would. It wasn't going to be an easy week. Biting his lip, he turned away to keep his scarlet face and glittering eyes and deep humiliation all to himself.

He found himself facing the corner window once again, where he had stood less than a week ago, clenching his fists in a fury and staring down at Flora's name, planted beyond the lake.

It was too dark to see anything now, except the sharpened dusk-blue reflection of four kind people waiting quietly, watching him in the same tell-tale pane of glass in which he was looking at them.

Flora and Riley, Chloe and Dr Barney.

They'll all be here, he told himself optimistically. I'll see them next week. I will have that to think about. And there's the play to cheer me up. Things could be worse.

He came across to say goodbye.

'See you next week,' he said to Dr Barney.

'I hope so, Ally,' Dr Barney said. 'Keep smiling.'

'Bye, Riley.'

Riley stuck out his hand. 'Thanks, Ally,' he said,

grinning encouragingly. 'Thank you for every-thing. See you next week.'

Ally gave Aunt Chloe a quick kiss on the cheek. 'Goodbye.' He didn't think that she'd be in the hospital much longer now. But still he promised her, 'I'll take you down there again soon. We'll have a picnic in the stone menagerie.'

She gave his hand a tiny, furtive squeeze.

He turned to Flora.

'See you on Sunday, Flora,' Ally said. 'Take care.'

She smiled at him and nodded. The little golden bells in her ears jangled away, giving him courage for the coming week.

Smiling as bravely as he could, he turned his back and left them.